CHILCOT'S REDEMPTION

Brook Chilcot's career as a sheriff ended after a disastrous shootout, and he is in no hurry to forgo his alcoholic haze. But when a young man wishing to be taught how to shoot convinces him to leave retirement, Brook returns to the town of Grafton's Peak, where he must deal with new faces and old enemies. As the son of an outlaw he killed many years ago arrives to confront him, Chilcot is given the chance to make up for his errors in the past. Will he take it?

ETHAN HARKER

CHILCOT'S REDEMPTION

Complete and Unabridged

LINFORD
Leicester

First published in Great Britain in 2015 by
Robert Hale Limited
London

First Linford Edition
published 2017
by arrangement with
Robert Hale
an imprint of The Crowood Press
Wiltshire

A catalogue record for this book is available
from the British Library.

ISBN 978-1-4448-3164-1

Published by
F. A. Thorpe (Publishing)
Anstey, Leicestershire

Set by Words & Graphics Ltd.
Anstey, Leicestershire
Printed and bound in Great Britain by
T. J. International Ltd., Padstow, Cornwall

This book is printed on acid-free paper

1

There was a new barkeep at the Girl of the Period; which circumstance gave Chilcot to hope that it might be worthwhile trying to extend his credit at the saloon. It was barely midday, but already Brook Chilcot felt a faint gnawing in the pit of his stomach. It was that old, familiar, nagging ache which would only be alleviated by a shot of ardent spirits.

The saloon wasn't crowded; most folk had better things to be doing at five minutes past noon on a Monday than getting liquored up in the Girl of the Period. There were only two men standing at the bar and another two or three seated at tables when Chilcot pulled open the batwing doors and walked in. He decided that a bold approach might pay off and so simply ordered a glass of whiskey; failing to mention, until it arrived, that he hadn't the cash money to pay for it. 'Just chalk it up on the slate, would you?' he said casually and reached down to scoop up the drink, before the man had had a chance to think the matter over.

The barkeep was too quick for him, though. He put out his hand and swiftly slid the glass back across the counter, saying, 'Sorry, Mr Chilcot. You owe a heap already. Boss says no more credit 'til you clear what's already owing.'

Upon hearing this blunt statement, two conflicting impulses arose and contended for mastery in Brook Chilcot's breast. The first of these was an almost overwhelming temptation to lean across the bar, grab hold of the young pup and then proceed to beat him to a pulp. Set in rivalry to this initial urge was that desperate longing for a gulp of strong liquor, which made him feel more like begging the fellow, with tears in his eyes, to allow him just this one glass. For a brief spell, Chilcot stood baffled; honestly unsure of what he would next do. He was unexpectedly rescued from the horns of his dilemma by one of the two men standing nigh to him at the bar, who leaned over and said, 'Here, let me get you that.' This fellow then handed over a few coins to the barkeep.

'Your very good health, sir,' said Chilcot gratefully.

The man smiled briefly, before turning back to his companion and saying, in what he evidently thought was too low a voice to be heard by the recipient of his charity, 'Poor old bastard. He used to be really something once upon a time, you know.'

Chilcot picked up the glass and took a sip. The golden liquid began working its magic almost immediately; the warm glow beginning in his belly and diffusing outwards from there. The pleasure was dulled somewhat, though, by the sting of that heedless remark. Still, he thought, as he took another sip of the whiskey, why should it hurt to hear the truth uttered? At sixty-six years of age, he surely was old by anyone's reckoning and he was certainly poor enough! As for being a bastard, well he would have to allow that there might be somewhat in that as well. Even so, it didn't make pleasant listening to have his character summed up so succinctly by a stranger. He guessed he would just have to swallow his pride and be grateful for the free drink.

Chilcot turned to survey the barroom. The two men standing near him were talking quietly together; it would probably be pointless to try to tap either of them for his next drink. There were two men seated together at one table and a single fellow at another. All three looked to be hard and uncompromising types, men who would be unlikely to take pity on an old soldier and retired lawman. Then the doors swung open and another person entered the saloon; a young man, scarcely more than a boy. This looked more promising.

The youth looked uncertainly round

the room before fixing his eyes on Chilcot and staring at him hard for a few seconds. Then, having apparently made up his mind, he walked over to the bar and said, 'Am I addressing Mr Brook W. Chilcot, by any chance?'

'Why yes, my boy. You surely are. Do I know you?'

'No sir, we never met. My father talked sometimes of you, though.'

'What was your father's name?'

'He was called David Pearson.'

Chilcot rubbed his chin thoughtfully and said, 'That don't bring anybody to mind.'

'Oh,' said the boy, 'you wouldn't have heard of him. He saw you shoot down some men one time in a gunfight. He said it was in 1867.'

'Yes, I'll allow that it's possible. I was mixed up in a lot of lively action that year. But suppose you tell me who you are and why you come looking for me?'

For answer, the young man reached into his jacket and extracted a folded-up copy of a newspaper. He handed this to Chilcot. As soon as he saw the name of the town on the masthead, Chilcot felt a shock of recognition. The paper was called the *Grafton's Peak Agricultural Gazette, Incorporating the Johnson County Intelligencer* and this issue was dated two weeks earlier; Monday, 6 May 1889. It was folded to show an article with the headline 'How the Mighty are Fallen!' Chilcot read the piece with considerable interest.

Our older readers may perhaps recall the name of BROOK W. CHILCOT; who, some years ago, was what might be termed a 'Big Wheel' in Grafton's Peak. Mr CHILCOT, sometime sheriff of the town, was credited with killing any number of supposed malefactors. It is, we concede, possible that some of his victims were themselves carrying firearms, although there were widespread and persistent rumours that this was not the case with all those gunned down by

Sheriff CHILCOT. It will be remembered that Sheriff CHILCOT, as he then was, was renowned both for his prowess with deadly weapons and also for an alarming tendency to inflict mortal wounds upon those whom another, less aggressive man might have brought in alive. These sanguinary exploits, which culminated in the massacre at the railroad station, did little to endear CHILCOT to many citizens of Grafton's Peak and when he left, the mourning at his departure was anything but universal. Word reaches us that the aforementioned CHILCOT is now 'down on his luck', as the saying goes. He is to be found in the Kansas town of Endurance, where he now gives full rein, when he can afford it, to that partiality for John Barleycorn, which was ever his besetting weakness. These days, we are given to understand, our former sheriff is more likely to provoke ridicule and mirth than he is the awe and respect in

7

which he was once held. Any readers of this newspaper who should ever chance to find themselves in Endurance are urged to behave like true Christians and hunt out CHILCOT and stand him a drink. They say in that town that if the poor fellow's circumstances do not soon improve, he might, before long, be reduced to hiring himself out as a night watchman or some similar lowly occupation.

Chilcot looked up sharply after finishing this far from flattering description of himself and said, 'Then what? You travel all the way from Grafton's Peak to show me this? Or are you planning to buy me a drink?'

'Neither, sir. The fellow as wrote that does not seem to like you overmuch.'

Chilcot, who had already noted and recognized the name of the man who had written the article, said, 'You got that right, son. I had to lock him up one time for drunkenness and although it was better than twenty years ago, he still ain't forgiven me by the sound of it. So what do you want?'

'I want you to teach me to shoot,' was the surprising reply.

Despite his longing for just one more drink, Chilcot thought that it might be politic to conceal this from the young fellow who was seemingly eager to hire him as a coach. He suggested that the two of them might take a turn up Main Street, so that the boy could fill him in on what he had in mind.

'It's like this, sir,' explained the boy, who revealed his name to be Jake Pearson. 'My ma, she runs a hardware store in Grafton's Peak. My pa died three years since, or happen we wouldn't find ourselves situated like we do. Meaning, he was a man who took care of matters and knew what was what.'

'Well,' said Chilcot, the effects of that first whiskey wearing off and the longing increasing in him for a second and third, 'what is this 'matter' of which you speak?'

'Some fellows in the town, hard men, you know, they've banded together to make money without working. Nobody knows the half o' what they're about, but just lately they hit upon a way of living at the expense of folk like my ma.'

'How so?'

'Some few months back, two of 'em came to the store and told Ma as they'd heard that there were some real bad types around who were planning to rob or harm the businesses in town. Said as they were offering to protect storekeepers and so on from these others. We heard where they'd been to see most every store, along of the blacksmith, undertaker, man in charge of the lumber mill and anybody else making regular money.'

Chilcot snorted. 'That's an old game,' he declared. 'That racket was old as the hills before the war. What happened next?'

'First off is where Ma turned them out of the store, told 'em they was a precious set of rascals and they'd not get a cent out of her by such tricks.'

'Did she, though?' asked Chilcot admiringly. 'Well then, I tell you, your ma's got more sand than most.'

'Didn't do her a mort o' good,' said Jake gloomily. 'All the other stores paid up. These men weren't askin' a ruinous amount of money. Fact is, Ma could've afforded to give it to them without it denting her profits too much. She's stubborn, though. But they came back again and now it looks like if she don't pay, there'll be trouble.'

'Ain't that the truth. Like I say, it's an old story. So what would you have of me?'

'They're leaning on my mother now, becoming more menacing. I think they're affeared as if one person refuses to pay up and nothing happens to 'em, then others'll feel the same way. I don't see that they'll let Ma get away much longer without paying them.'

'It's a sad story,' said Chilcot patiently, 'but I still don't see where I enter into the picture.'

'I'll pay you to teach me how to use a gun. Then I can stand up to those bullies and show 'em as they ought to leave my ma alone.'

The old man stopped dead in his tracks and turned to stare at the youngster. 'Boy, that road needs a lot of thought, 'fore you set out along it. How old are you?'

'Eighteen, this month gone.'

'I'd o' thought you was younger than that. You're small for your age. You know the names of any o' these villains? And what's the sheriff a-thinkin' of, putting up with such goings on?'

'As for names, the leader of the crew is a fellow called Catesby. Matt Catesby. Do you know the name?'

'Can't say as I do. It's been some years since I was down that way, it's not in reason that I should recognize too many of the younger men. What about the sheriff?'

'My ma says as he's the worst of the lot. She thinks he's either in cahoots with the gang or taking bribes or something of the sort. His name's Tranter, Keith Tranter.'

'Tranter, you say,' said Chilcot, turning sharply to look at the young man. 'Keith Tranter? Tell me, this wouldn't be a fellow about . . . ' he thought for a moment, 'say thirty years of age, maybe a little more? Black hair with very pale blue eyes? Striking-looking, stares at you like a snake?'

'Why yes, that's a good enough description of Sheriff Tranter. You know him?'

'I knew him as a boy. That's over twenty years ago, though. His anteced-ents weren't what you might call promising, if this is the same fellow.'

'I make no doubt it is, else you couldn't o' told just what he looks like. How'd you know him?'

'That's nothing to the purpose. Listen, son, I need to think about this for a spell. You have somewhere to stay in this town?'

'No, I came straight to the saloon, on account of that's where folk I asked at the depot said you'd most likely be found.'

'Tell you what, if I go along with your scheme or not, you'll still need a place to lay your head tonight. Walk straight down this here road and you'll come to a big house at the end, on the right. Painted white, with camellias growing by the door. They rent out rooms for the night there. I'll come by the place in an hour or so and we'll see what's to do.'

The youngster appeared reluctant to go off alone, but Chilcot could be mighty pushing when he'd a mind to be. After young Pearson had gone, Chilcot found a spot under a tall, spreading oak tree; a favourite resting place of his, where somebody had thoughtfully set a log so that passersby could take the weight off their feet. He sat down there and thought over what the boy had told him.

Could it really be that Ike Adams's boy had risen to be sheriff of the town his father had once troubled? Tranter was an unusual name and it was this which the half-breed squaw with whom Ike Adams had picked up called herself: Hettie Tranter. Their boy had been called Keith and how many Keith Tranters were there likely to be in that corner of Texas? No, that was the same boy, for a bet. Chilcot closed his eyes and let his mind drift back over twenty years to the time when he had himself been the sheriff of Grafton's Peak.

He recalled clearly the first time that he crossed swords with one of the Adams brothers. It had been almost six months after he had been sworn in as sheriff of Grafton's Peak, and what a hard row to hoe that had turned out to be! Chilcot was the first sheriff the town had had; a vigilance committee having previously maintained order. As the place grew, though, having a bunch of men hand out beatings and arrange the occasional hanging was not really sufficient. Somebody was needed to collect taxes, issue permits, check up on liquor licensing and a host of other petty jobs that could hardly be undertaken by a mob of citizenry acting chiefly by night. And so the town had engaged Chilcot to keep order and supervise all the things that needed to be done in a civilized community.

From the beginning, the four Adams brothers were a thorn in Chilcot's side. They had arrived in Grafton's Peak a few months after the surrender was signed at Appomattox Courthouse; paying in gold for an old farmhouse up in the hills, some three miles from town. Their names were Ike, short for Isaac, Jethro, Moses and Ezra. Folk said their parents must have been right devout to name all their sons from Scripture.

How the brothers made their money was not plain; it certainly wasn't from farming. Chilcot's guess was that they did a bit of everything, from moonshining to running guns into the Indian Nations. As long as their activities were conducted away from town, he didn't see that he was called upon to take any official notice of them. Came the day though, when Ike Adams and his brothers began to throw their weight about in town and that was a thing which Sheriff Chilcot was not about to endure.

They began in a small way, by putting the bite on the owner of a saloon; demanding free drinks in exchange for 'helping out'. This 'helping out' consisted in the chief of their being supplied with liquor in return for not starting fights with the other patrons of the Golden Eagle and smashing the place up. Not wishing to be thought of as a tale-bearer, the owner approached Chilcot privately about this and he promised to look into it.

That evening, Sheriff Chilcot was standing at the bar of the Golden Eagle, enjoying a quiet drink, when in walked Ike Adams. He ordered a whiskey, picked it up and turned to move away from the bar. Chilcot said, 'You going to pay for that drink?'

'What's it to you?'

'Just answer the question, Adams.'

Ike Adams said nothing, but reached into a pocket and withdrew a handful of coins, which he dumped contemptuously on the counter before stalking off to join some friends at a table. He had not even looked at Chilcot during the brief exchange, but the sheriff sensed that he had made an enemy. Ike Adams and his brothers now knew that whatever they got up to up in the mountains or across the line in the Indian Territories, the sheriff of Grafton's Peak was not going to allow any carryings-on in the town itself.

Somebody was shaking Chilcot by the shoulder and for a moment, he didn't know where he was. So vivid had the dream been, that he thought he was still in the Golden Eagle. The fellow who had been shaking him said, 'You all right, old-timer? Lord, I thought you'd upped an' died on us there, you were that still.'

'No, I'm still in the land of the living.

Just catching a catnap. But I'm obliged to you for your concern.'

After the man had gone, Chilcot sat under the old oak tree, reflecting upon his memories. This was not the first time lately that he had moved seamlessly from daydreaming to actual dreaming sleep and been unaware of the transition. Maybe, he thought, it is the kind of thing that happens to you as you grow old. The memories of Grafton's Peak were now as fresh in his mind as though they were from yesterday and not better than twenty years ago. Then he suddenly recollected that he had agreed to meet that boy at the lodging house. He looked down the street to the clock above the courthouse and was relieved to see that it still lacked a few minutes to one.

Jake Pearson was pleased and relieved when he glanced from the window and saw the old man approaching down the street. 'Old' was certainly the word for the fellow, thought Jake. His hair and mustache were snowy white and he walked with that painstaking care that a lot of old people did; like he was affeared of tumbling into a pit or something. Could this man really be the fearsome Brook Chilcot, whose actions were still spoken of with awe, the better part of a quarter century later? The boy's heart misgave him and he wondered if he'd taken a wrong turn in coming haring up here to Kansas without so much as a by-your-leave from his mother. Well, he was here now and he had made an offer to the former sheriff of Grafton's Peak. The only honourable thing to do was to go through with his plan and see what might develop from it.

2

It wasn't often these days that Chilcot went heeled. It had been some little while since he'd had cause to defend himself against any deadly assault and in any case, the sight of an old gentleman like him, sporting a gun at his hip, was likely to provoke amusement these days, rather than healthy respect. It wasn't only his age, of course. It was becoming increasingly rare generally to see men carrying firearms, unless they were going hunting. Times were changing.

He supposed that there would be no harm in giving a few shooting lessons to a young man. The chances of this youth actually using the skills thus acquired to kill a man were slender and it would be good, thought Chilcot, to supplement the tiny pension upon which he was almost wholly reliant these days. The gun and holster were kept in the trunk beneath his bed. Chilcot pulled this out and removed the tooled, black leather rig which once had been a permanent feature of his dress. The pistol was packed separately; wrapped carefully in greaseproof paper. How long had it been since he had worn the thing? Six months? A year? Maybe more?

Nearly every pistol that one saw today was double action; that is to say that pulling on the trigger both raised and then let fall the hammer. Chilcot had never favoured such weapons, finding that the muscular pressure required to bring up the hammer tended to spoil his aim. With this gun, which was an old cap and ball Navy Colt, you needs must first cock the hammer and then the merest touch on the trigger would cause the thing to fire. This one had been modified years ago, so as to make it even more sensitive. Chilcot had filed down the notch inside the handle where the hammer caught. It was that narrow now that he had in the past boasted that once cocked, a fly settling on the trigger would be enough to fire the piece.

Buckling on the gunbelt was a sobering experience for the old man. True, he was only going to give some fool-boy a lesson in marksmanship, but the weight of the gun pressing against his hip always served as a reminder to Chilcot that he was now ready and able to deal out death, should need arise. He smiled and said quietly, 'That's a lot of foolishness. You're knocking on seventy, Chilcot. You need to recollect your age and start thinking on the world to come.'

The boy was waiting out front of the house. He was carrying a carpet bag and looked less dangerous than any man Brook Chilcot had ever set eyes on in the whole course of his life. The idea of this young innocent planning to brace Ike Adams's son brought a smile to Chilcot's lips. The youngster was watching him and so he suppressed the amusement he felt and became instead brisk and businesslike. 'You got your piece in that there bag, have you? Good man.'

They collected Chilcot's horse from the field at back of the livery stable. The plan was to go up into the hills surrounding the town and find a nice, quiet spot to try a little shooting. As they walked through town, it struck Chilcot that he hadn't yet established just exactly how much Pearson was prepared to pay for the privilege of receiving tuition from a man who was once renowned as the fastest shot in three states. Well, the youth didn't look like a hard bargainer and there would be time enough later to dicker over terms.

'You don't mind a walk, I guess?' asked Chilcot. 'I can't go as far on Shank's pony as once I was able, so you won't feel it unfair if I ride while you go afoot?'

'Not a bit of it, sir,' said the young man politely. 'Tell you the truth, it feels good to stretch my limbs on such a day as this. I spend a deal of time cooped up indoors and I'm always glad to get out in the fresh air.'

'That's the spirit.'

After collecting his mare and tacking her up, Chilcot directed them back along Main Street; he riding and the boy walking alongside him. A peculiarity of his mount was that while she was as steady as you like under most any unexpected circumstance, she could not abide bicycles. There was something about the rapidly spinning, shiny wheels and the imperious ringing of their bells which served always to put the horse out of countenance. After she had jittered away for the third or fourth time, Jake Pearson ventured to observe, 'Your horse seems right nervous, sir.'

'Nervous?' exclaimed Chilcot indignantly. 'Don't presume to say so! She's as steady as a rock under gunfire, thunder, lightning or pretty much anything else, excepting these blamed bicycles. Something about them spooks her.'

Once they were a few miles from the town limits, Chilcot led them off the road and into a little wood. When they reached a glade, he dismounted and said, 'Now you'll see whether this beast o' mine is nervous or not.' Without any warning, he drew his pistol, cocking it with his thumb as he did so, and fired at once. The youth at his side flinched, but the horse remained as untroubled as though the sudden roar of the gun were no more to her than the buzzing of a fly. 'There now,' said Chilcot proudly, 'you want to talk about nervous horses at all?'

After replacing the gun in his holster, Chilcot said, 'All right, let's see what you have.' The boy looked puzzled and so he elaborated, 'Your piece. What are you carrying?'

'Oh, you mean my gun? Here it is.' Pearson opened that ridiculous carpet bag and withdrew a revolver. He handled it gingerly, like it might go off at any moment. Straight away, it was as plain as a pikestaff to Chilcot that this fellow had not had any sort of experience with guns.

'First things, first,' said Chilcot, 'you ever fire any sort of weapon? Other than a slingshot?'

'No sir, my ma is dead set against guns. She's a Quaker. I'm supposed to be too, but I reckon as there's times when you got to bend your principles.'

'Could be you're right. Anyways, why don't I show you first how we go about the business?'

The gun that Jake Pearson had brought along with him was a Colt 1878, the double-action army model. Try as he might, Chilcot had never been able to get used to using brass cartridges, rather than filling chambers with loose powder and so he looked a little askance at the pistol. Nevertheless, it seemed a workmanlike weapon and the feel of it in his hand was fine. 'Where'd you come by this?' he asked. 'Thought your ma didn't hold with such things.'

'Borrowed it.'

It took no time at all to discover that Jake Pearson was utterly hopeless with guns and that the idea of him pulling a pistol and standing up to some gang was a mere pipe dream. Chilcot had suspicioned so from the off and the half-hour that the two of them spent in that clearing served only to confirm strongly his initial doubts. He had no desire to shame the boy, but it would be sheer murder to let him leave here with the hope of facing men who most likely relied upon firearms for their living. Some of what he was thinking was evidently written on his face, because young Pearson looked anxiously at him and said, 'I know I'll need a good deal more practice, but I'll do all right, won't I, sir?'

Instead of answering directly, Chilcot asked, 'How long do you aim to be spending here in Endurance?'

'I don't want to be away for too long. I don't know what those fellows purpose next, you see. Ma's all alone without me.'

'Tell you what, young fellow,' said Chilcot kindly, 'why don't we forget about all this for now and then see how things stand in the morning, when I've had a chance to think it all over a bit. How does that sound?'

'It's good of you to take the trouble, sir. How much do I owe you for this afternoon's teaching?'

'You don't owe me a cent. Not yet, at any rate.'

After they got back to town and Chilcot had made an excuse to escape from the youth's company, he realized something very curious. He'd not thought at all of alcohol since first he'd spoken to Jake Pearson. Which was decidedly odd, because in the normal way of things, after that first drink of the day he thought of little else than where the next whiskey was coming from. Maybe it was having something to think about for a change; another person's problems, other than his own, to consider.

At about this time of day, Chilcot was

29

accustomed to lying on his bed and resting for a little. In a way, he wished that he had not recommended the same lodging house where he was himself staying when suggesting somewhere for the youngster to stay. Luckily, he managed to slip in and get to his room without encountering either Jake Pearson or the widow who ran the place. Chilcot kicked off his boots, unbuckled his gun and lay down on the bed. The dream he had had earlier that day about meeting Ike Adams in the Golden Eagle all those years ago had somehow stuck in his mind. He closed his eyes and consciously turned his mind back in time, to the events of that late summer of 1867.

From that moment in the saloon, when he'd forced Ike Adams to pay for his drink, Chilcot knew that he had been marked by the Adams brothers as an enemy to whom they owed a bad turn. There were plenty in town who didn't care overmuch for their sheriff to begin with. For one thing, he was a

Yankee and almost to a man, the citizens of Grafton's Peak had favoured the Confederacy from that first fateful day when the Yankees were shelled out of Fort Sumter. He had been engaged by the vigilance committee because they knew of his solid background in law-keeping and because they thought that an older man — he was at that time already forty-four — would be a calming influence. What he hadn't known when he took up the post was that he would be expected to turn a blind eye to some things and, above all, not to make ructions.

A couple of days after the incident in the Golden Eagle, Sheriff Chilcot had cause to reprove another of the Adams brothers. In fairness to Ezra Adams, he was the youngest and probably the least troublesome of the four. He couldn't have been above twenty years of age when he fell out with Chilcot.

One of the reasons that Brook W. Chilcot had succeeded in living past his forty-fourth birthday, despite having been a soldier and lawman for better than twenty-five years, was that he had a very keenly tuned sense of danger. There were those who swore that Chilcot must have eyes in the back of his neck; he was that quick to react to the threat of death. This was one of those times when, even though there was no apparent threat in the here and now, Chilcot was aware that there were four men hanging round that town who would most likely contrive to see him killed if they believed that he was liable to act as a check upon their activities.

Having twisted Ike Adams's tail, Chilcot knew damned well that he'd best keep a watch out for the other three brothers as well. He also made a private oath to come down right sharpish on the first sign of anything which smacked to him of disrespect towards either him personally or for the law; in Chilcot's mind, the two were more or less indistinguishable. So it was that when he saw Ezra Adams hawk

and spit on the boardwalk one afternoon a few days after his little run-in
with Ike, Chilcot thought he should set
the young man on the right path. This
was especially so, since the boy had spat
right in front of the sheriff, as they were
approaching each other. Chilcot moved
swiftly in front of Ezra Adams to block
his path and said, 'That's one filthy
habit, you know that? Not to mention
that there's a bye-law against disorderly
conduct of that kind. Don't you let me
see you spit like that again, you hear
what I'm tellin' you?'

The young fellow looked surprised
and then, because others were watching
to see what would happen next and he
didn't want to lose face, he cleared his
throat and spat again; the phlegm
splattering Chilcot's boots. The sheriff
didn't say anything or look the least bit
annoyed. He half turned away and
then, as quick as a rattlesnake, he
grabbed a hold of Ezra Adams's
shirtfront and whirled him round;
running him backward until he banged

into the nearby wall. Then, before the boy had a chance to react, Chilcot snatched the pistol from his holster and threw it to one side. After that, he neatly and expertly twisted the young man's arm up behind his back and frogmarched him down Main Street to his office.

When they got to the sheriff's office, Chilcot kicked open the door and then gave Ezra an almighty great shove, sending the young man sprawling onto the floor. Still not allowing him any time to figure out what was happening, Chilcot hauled him to his feet and then pushed him to the back of the room, where half of the office had been converted into a cell by the simple addition of bars running from floor to ceiling. The sheriff locked him in the cell and then said, 'Here's how things stand, boy. I ain't about to have either you or any of those brothers of yours struttin' around this town, setting my authority at nought. I won't have it and the sooner you and they know it, the better.'

'Wait 'til my brothers catch a hold of you. You'll see all about your precious authority bein' set at nought.'

'They know where I am. Listen, now. I'm fining you five dollars for disorderly conduct. You got that much about you?'

Ezra Adams stared at the sheriff as if he'd taken leave of his senses. 'You say what?' he exclaimed. 'You ain't serious 'bout that?'

'Look at my face now,' advised Chilcot, 'and tell me if'n I look like a man who's joshing. You'll always know when I'm not being serious. That'd be when I slap on a bit of greasepaint, like a circus clown, and cut a caper. You see any sign of that right now?'

'I ain't got no five dollars on me, so what're you goin' to do?'

'You can spend a night here instead of the fine, if you'd rather.'

Like all the Adams brothers, Ezra's fuse was none too long. He said, 'Ah, come on man. Quit fooling round. You can't lock me up just for spittin' on the boardwalk. I never heard the like!'

'You heard it now.'

There was a method in Chilcot's apparent madness in bating the Adams brothers in this way by seizing the youngest of them on a flimsy pretext and it was this. It was obvious to him that sooner or later there would be a confrontation of some kind between him and the four brothers. They were spending more and more time in town and behaving in ways that made it clear that they were trying to lean on some of those living in Grafton's Peak. Chilcot was lancing the boil; ensuring that when the confrontation erupted, it would be on his terms and not theirs; at a time and place of his own choosing.

While he was bandying words with the youngest of the Adams brothers, the door to the street opened and a man poked his head in. He said, 'Sheriff, thought I'd warn you. Somebody told Ike Adams about what happened with you and his kid brother. Him, Jethro and Moses are heading this way and they ain't none too happy from what I saw.'

'I'm obliged to you for the information. You best make yourself scarce now; you don't want to be near here when they arrive.'

'I done told you,' said Ezra triumphantly. 'I said as they wouldn't be happy with you. Why'nt you turn me loose now, afore they get here?'

'Not in a million years,' said Chilcot, going to a stout closet set against the wall. He produced a key from his pocket and then opened the closet door. From within, he took a double-barrelled, sawn-off scattergun and a box of copper caps. He fitted two of these over the nipples beneath the hammers and then replaced the box in the closet; carefully locking the door when he had done so. Then he walked slowly over to the door leading out onto Main Street and waited for the three brothers to come.

Chilcot opened his eyes with a start, aware that he had been dozing. For a second, he was disoriented and then recollected that he had been sleeping in the afternoon. This often left him momentarily confused, when first he woke. The effect of that single glass of whiskey, which he had had earlier, had worn off and he felt more clear-headed than he generally did at this time of day.

The sleep had done Chilcot good, because he knew now where his duty lay. He would have to tell that eager young man that he should under no circumstances consider setting himself in opposition to some armed criminal. It would be suicide. It was a nuisance, because Chilcot could surely have done with a little extra money, but he would not have been able to live with himself had he given that lad to believe that he would be able to handle himself against a real gunfighter; a man who had, most likely, grown up with firearms. This was to say nothing of Ike Adams's son being somehow mixed up in the affair. The good Lord alone knew what was going on in that town these days.

Having made this decision there was little point in not communicating it to the boy at once. The sooner he gave up his mad plans, the better it would be for him. Chilcot pulled on his boots and left the room. There had been only one unoccupied room in the house that morning, which was the one where young Jake Pearson was doubtless now lodged. Chilcot went across the landing and rapped smartly on the door. The youngster called for him to come in and Chilcot did so.

The boy was sitting at the small table, which was spread with various papers and books. He hurriedly began to pack these away, but not before Chilcot had picked up one of the books and examined it. It was a guide to algebra.

'Ciphering a hobby o' yours or something?' asked the old man and then the truth struck him and he said, 'Ah, Jeez. Tell me you're not still at school, surely? How old are you again?'

'Almost eighteen.'

'Almost? How old are you really?'

'Old enough to take care of my ma.'

'Quit fooling now. Tell me how old you are.'

'Fifteen, going on sixteen.'

Even though he'd now guessed that this might be the case, Chilcot was appalled. 'God almighty son, whatever ails you that you should tell me such a big lie about being eighteen? Does your ma even know where you are?'

'I'm boarding at school. She saw me off at the railroad station and I just switched trains and came here to find you, 'stead o' going back to school.'

'Lord a mercy,' muttered Chilcot and sat down on the bed to recover. One thing was certain; he would have to return this foolish child to his home and that right away. He could see that nothing else would meet the case. Looking up at Jake Pearson, he said, 'This is a damned nuisance, you know that? A damned nuisance.'

'I don't see that it's any of your affair. I came here by my own self and I guess

I can leave town in the same way, if you ain't a-going to aid me.'

'Not while I got breath in my body, you don't,' said Chilcot firmly. 'I can't let a child go wandering off without taking steps to ensure that he's safe. No, there's nothing for it, you and me'll have to travel back to Grafton's Peak in each other's company.'

The boy pulled a woebegone face, whereupon Chilcot felt sorry for him. He said quietly, 'I can see you meant well, but it won't answer. You'll never be any great shakes with a gun, I can tell you that. You stick to arithmetic and such for now. Come, it ain't as bad as all that. Did you come up on the Katy Flyer?'

'Yes sir, that I did.'

'Well then, we can go back on the same track. Mind, I don't have the wherewithal for a ticket, so I reckon as we'll have to spend that money you were goin' to pay me for shooting lessons to book me a passage south.'

3

Although he had told young Jake that it was a nuisance for him to be compelled to travel down to Grafton's Peak, the truth was that Chilcot was not at all averse to the trip. He seldom went more than a few miles from Endurance these days and the idea of a long railroad journey was an enticing one in some ways. The Katy Flyer stopped off at Endurance before heading south through the Indian Nations into Texas. They would have to change onto a little local service in order to get to Grafton's Peak, but other than that, it was a straightforward and uncomplicated route.

It was sheer vanity, but Chilcot had resolved to wear his gun on the way down to Grafton's Peak. He did so not because he expected any sort of trouble, but rather because he was getting on in years and he thought that by being heeled he would cut a rather more dignified figure in the town where he had once ruled the roost. He didn't want to appear in the character of an old has-been.

When he and the boy were settled in their seats on the train next day, Chilcot said, 'I surely hope that your mother will not be too anxious about you, son. I dare say as your school will've telegraphed her by now and told her that you didn't make it there. She'll like as not be plumb distracted with worry.'

'I never thought of that,' said the young man frankly. 'I wouldn't o' got her fretting so for all the world.' He looked anxious at the idea.

'Ain't it always the way? Young folk never stop to think how they're causin' trouble for others.' Then, seeing that the boy really was worried about his mother, Chilcot added, 'Lord, don't take on so. You did what you thought was best for your ma. It does you credit, even if it was the craziest scheme

43

I ever did hear of. Don't you worry now; I'll speak to your ma and explain that you meant well. It'll be fine.'

'Why are you taking such care of me, sir? It ain't like we're related or nothing.'

'I'd never sleep easy in my bed again if I just let you go off by yourself. It was a hazardous enough undertaking to come all the way up here by yourself. I couldn't let you go back alone.'

Jake Pearson looked as though he was the type to chat all the way through a train journey, which didn't at all accord with the way that Chilcot liked to arrange matters. He said to the boy, 'Anyways, that'll be about enough gossip for now. I aim to have a little sleep. It's a long way and I always like to close my eyes for as much of the time as I might. You got your school books in that bag?'

'Yes sir.'

'Well then I reckon the best thing as you can do is catch up on some of the lessons you missed by coming traipsing up here to see me.'

Chilcot did not wait for any reply, but leaned back in the seat and closed his eyes.

Although he was tired and the motion of the railroad train soporific, Chilcot found himself unable to sleep. It was strange that he found himself heading down to Grafton's Peak after all these years. Who would have forseen such a thing a week ago? Such was life; you never really knew what it was going to throw at you next.

Grafton's Peak! And with Ike Adams's boy running the place as sheriff; that was the strangest thing Chilcot had ever heard tell of. The folk in that town must have taken leave of their senses to agree to such an arrangement. Ike Adams's boy . . . Inevitably, Chilcot found his thoughts turning to that day in his office, the day that set everything on the path to that disastrous showdown.

Sheriff Chilcot glanced through the window and saw the three Adams brothers walking slowly up the street towards his office. They were walking close together, side by side, and Chilcot hoped that they would continue in that way until they reached him. He drew back the hammers on the scattergun and looked at the weapon, trying to gauge what the spread of the shot would be at a distance of thirty feet or so. Ten feet, maybe? Then he strolled over to the door leading out onto Main Street and opened it. He raised the sawn-off shotgun to his shoulder and stood there, just inside the doorway; out of sight from without until you were standing in the street, right in front of the door.

Ike, Moses and Jethro sauntered along in the middle of the road until they reached the sheriff's office. Then they turned to face the wooden building, which was all but indistinguishable from the stores lining the boardwalk. It was only at that point that they caught sight of Brook W. Chilcot, standing in the shadows. He advanced slowly towards them and it wasn't until he stepped out into the sunlight that they realized that he had a weapon at his shoulder and was drawing down on them.

''Fore any o' you boys make any sudden moves,' said Chilcot pleasantly, 'let me tell you how things stand. I got this sawn-off loaded with a heap of bits o' iron. Screws, tin-tacks and I don't know what all else. I got it double charged too. At this range, I'll take oath that if I let fly with both barrels, I'll kill two o' you instantly and most likely give a mortal wound to the third.'

Chilcot gave the three men time to digest his words. Say what you would about the Adams brothers, but they weren't fools. They could see that he had most likely taken first pull on the triggers and that even if by some miracle, one of them was fast enough to draw and shoot him, that he would still be able to fire in his final moments. They'd all of them seen the damage a scattergun was capable of causing to the human body at that range and, as Chilcot had said, the spread at that distance would like as not catch the three of them.

'Hell,' said Ike Adams mildly, 'we only come here to talk. There's no call for this.'

'You talk away now,' replied Chilcot, 'I'm a-listenin'.'

'We hear where you got our baby brother locked up there on some piss-ant charge, something 'bout spittin' on the boardwalk.'

'You heard right, Ike. So what was it you had to say on that subject?'

'Ah, come on. You can't lock up a man for spitting. You must be crazy.'

'Yeah,' said Chilcot, 'let's say as I'm crazy.'

'So what's it to be?' asked Moses. 'You goin' to fight to the death over this, or what?'

Chilcot was aware that ordinary life on Main Street had come to a halt and that a crowd of interested observers were following his exchanges with the

Adams brothers. This was good, because his aim was to put them in their place and show that the slightest infringement of the law would bring down his wrath upon their heads. The sheriff said, 'Fight to the death? Over spitting on the boardwalk? Now who's talkin' crazy? Really, you fellows must o' been out in the sun too long! No, it's a five dollar fine. Either that or a night in gaol.'

Hearing the case set out in such trifling terms was irking the three men standing in front of Chilcot's office and they looked as though they felt that they were being made fools of. This was good, because that was precisely Sheriff Chilcot's aim. He said, 'Listen, boys, you want to pay your brother's fine for him, he can walk free this very minute. Of course, if you all can't raise five dollars between you . . . ' There were chuckles from the watching crowd at this.

Ike Adams's hand began moving towards his pocket, whereupon Chilcot tensed and told him, 'You stop moving. It's making me nervous and if I make any kind o' mistake with this here scattergun, we'll not be able to set it right in this world.'

Instantly, Ike froze. He said, 'You want five dollars, how am I to take it from my pocket?'

'You're not,' replied Chilcot. 'Let your brother Jethro there reach into your pocket slowly with his left hand. I don't want to see anybody's right hand move, else I'll get twitchy and we don't none of us want that, I reckon.'

Very slowly, Jethro Adams dipped his hand into his brother's pocket and extracted a handful of coins. He said to Chilcot, 'If'n you don't want me to use my right hand, how'd you expec' me to count out five dollars?'

'Just let those dollars drop to the road, one by one. Do it five times and there we are.'

When his instructions had been followed, Chilcot told the three men, 'I'll pick that up directly. In the meanwhile, I'm going to go into the office and let your brother out. Don't none of you boys move a muscle, though, while I'm a-doin' of it. I can see you all well enough through the door.' Having said which, he backed slowly into the office, covering them the whole time with his scattergun. Once he was in the shadows, he took out the key and unlocked the barred door to the little cell, saying to Ezra Adams, 'You're free to go, boy.' He never once lowered the weapon from his shoulder or took his eyes from the men standing in the street outside.

Once the young man had left the cell and was walking out into the street, Chilcot followed him from behind and took up his position again, aiming in the general direction of the Adams brothers. It looked like most every citizen in Grafton's Peak had gathered to watch the sheriff lay down the law to the Adams boys and many folk thought that there might yet still be gunplay. The moment had passed, though, and both the sheriff and the four men standing outside his office knew it. That there would be a later reckoning for these actions of his seemed inevitable, but for now the tension had ebbed away. The four brothers turned and left without speaking another word to Chilcot. When once they were out of sight, he walked down off the step and collected the five dollars, where it was lying in the dust.

* * *

'Mr Chilcot, sir. I say, are you asleep, sir?'

Chilcot opened his eyes and discovered that the train was no longer moving and that he must, after all, have dozed off. 'Well, what is it, son?' he asked crankily. 'You best have a good reason for disturbin' my slumbers.'

'I'm sorry, sir, only I think there's some kind o' trouble.'

'Trouble? How so?'

'Well, as we were coming up the

incline, the train stopped all of a sudden. It was like somebody had pulled the emergency brake. Then there was some shoutin' up by the locomotive and there's some riders up there. Look, you can see them from here.'

Chilcot was sitting, as was his custom, with his back to the engine. He craned his neck round and peered along the tracks. The boy was right; there were two riders there, with two spare horses along of them. The most disquieting circumstance was that the men had bandannas tied round the lower half of their faces. There was not the slightest doubt in the old man's mind that they were up to some species of villainy.

'Ah, shit!' muttered Chilcot, before recollecting that he was in the presence of a minor. He added hastily, 'Sorry, son, it just slipped out. This really is a facer.'

'What shall we do?' asked Jake Pearson nervously.

'Do?' exclaimed Chilcot in surprise.

'We don't 'do' anything. Just sit tight and see what develops. Like enough, those boys are after something in the rear coach. You'll see, they won't trouble us.'

Although he had spent much of his life as a peace officer and was as shrewd a man as one could hope to find, Brook Chilcot was hopelessly wrong on this occasion. In his younger days, train robberies had been important affairs, when a well organized gang of determined robbers might hold up a railroad train to seize a cargo of bullion or some similarly valuable haul. These days, most of the country was civilized and law-abiding and there were only shrinking pockets of territory where you might be able to pull off a robbery of that sort. The outlaws who hid out in the Indian Nations were often just two-bit thieves, who would, from time to time, stop a passing train just to see what they could steal from passengers in the way of watches, billfolds and jewellery.

The former sheriff was accordingly the most relaxed man on the train as the three men climbed aboard with drawn pistols. He honestly did not believe that this robbery would concern him or any of the other passengers.

Leaving one of their company to hold the driver and stoker at gunpoint, preventing them from getting the locomotive moving again before the robbery was completed, the three other members of the band moved slowly down the train. They had taken the precaution of shooting up the telegraph wires running alongside the track and were feeling pretty confident of being able to take all that they required and be away from the scene long before anybody was able to muster a posse or rouse any lawmen.

One of the men carried a large leather satchel, into which was tossed the wallets of the men and any of the women's jewellery to which they took a fancy. They moved easily through the first two coaches and it wasn't until they reached the third, where Chilcot and his young friend were seated, that things went wrong.

As a sheriff, Chilcot had always had a certain grudging respect for those who made their living by knocking over banks or holding up trains. It took some daring to undertake crimes of that sort and although he would hunt down the perpetrators ruthlessly, he still acknowledged that they were men; men whose lives had taken a different course to his own. It was almost as though he and the outlaws of that sort were playing the same game but found themselves on opposing teams. By contrast, he felt nothing but loathing for those who preyed on women and other helpless folk. To Brook Chilcot, these types were like dogs and he would hunt them down and, if necessary, shoot them out of hand.

So it was that when he had learned that the train on which he was a passenger was being robbed, Chilcot had cheerfully sat back and resolved to take no part in the proceedings. He assumed that either there would be some guard to deal with a robbery from a secure coach at back of the train, or at worst, lawmen would track down the criminals at a later date. In either case, an old man like him did not need to stir his self up about the business.

As the three robbers entered the coach in which Chilcot was sitting, though, he realized that he had mistaken the nature of their crime. Nobody appeared to be stopping these fellows from making off with the money of a lot of ordinary people and, to Chilcot's way of thinking, that wasn't right. Even then, he was in two minds about what he should do; hoping that he could just sit tight and continue his journey once these scoundrels had accomplished their purpose.

Having established that he neither wished, nor was duty-bound, to do anything, Chilcot heard a woman behind him saying in great distress, 'Oh, please don't take my earbobs!

They were my late mother's and I set a store by them. Look, I'll give you this locket instead.'

A rough voice said, 'We'll have the locket too, lady, but you just unfasten those earbobs, 'fore I rip 'em from your ears.'

'You don't understand . . . ' began the woman, who sounded to Chilcot to be on the same side of sixty as he was himself. Then she gave a cry of pain. Looking round, he saw that one of the men had banged her over the head with his gun and now looked as though he were getting ready to pistol-whip her into submission, should she not comply immediately with his demands. Chilcot leaned over to the boy sitting opposite him and said quietly, 'You set right here and don't move a muscle; you hear what I tell you?'

To Jake Pearson's amazement, the white-haired old man stood up and walked towards the men who were working their way down the coach. All three of them had kerchiefs pulled up over their mouths and noses; all of them were holding guns. The youngster's mouth was dry with fear; he fully expected to see the former sheriff of Grafton's Peak get himself gunned down on the spot. As for the robbers, they couldn't make out the play at all. Coming towards them was an elderly-looking party with snow-white hair and mustache; an old fellow of the type you might think to see sitting on his porch in a rocking chair of an evening. He was dressed in sober and clerical-looking black and his long jacket concealed from sight the pistol at his hip.

'What d'you want, old man?' asked one of them. 'You best go and sit back down in your seat. Don't worry, we'll be along directly to relieve you of your money.' He turned to his companions and said, 'Lord, some o' the folk on this here train are in a rare hurry to have us rob them!' The other two men chuckled at this.

'I think you men should leave that lady alone,' said Chilcot politely. 'You surely don't need to take those earbobs of hers. Haven't you got enough now? Tell you what, why don't you just take what you already have and leave now?'

There was a gale of laughter from all three of the men, who seemed to be genuinely amused by what Chilcot said. At length, they recovered themselves and the one who had struck the woman said, 'Get along now and go back to your seat, or we might get irate with you. Go on, old man, get your arse back there, before you get yourself hurt.'

Jake Pearson could not tear his eyes away from the scene unfolding before him. He wished that old Mr Chilcot would just come back and sit down; he was surely going to get himself hurt if he carried on bandying words with those outlaws. Apart from his concern for the old lawman, Jake was finding the whole episode unbelievably thrilling. It was like one of his dime novels come to life. As he watched, Mr Chilcot turned away from the three robbers, his shoulders hunched over and looking like a whipped puppy. He said something that sounded to the boy like, 'Well, have it your own way.' It was an enormous relief to Jake to see that Chilcot had seemingly decided that discretion was, on this occasion at least, the better part of valour. Then he saw the old man's face and knew that the last thing on Brook W. Chilcot's mind was coming back to his seat.

As he turned, as those boys thought, to slink back to his seat and wait there quietly to be robbed, Chilcot heard the mocking laughs of the men who thought that they could now continue with their beastliness. He felt almost sorry for them; they probably hadn't been in this kind of business half as long as he had. As he turned to the right and made as though to walk off, Chilcot reached down casually and drew the Navy Colt which hung heavy and reassuring at his hip. He drew back the hammer and cocked the piece with his thumb as he pulled it from the holster. The men behind him couldn't see what he was about, because he had his back to them. Then, without moving particularly fast or doing anything liable to arouse their apprehensions, Chilcot turned back to face them; his pistol in his hand, pointing straight at the man who had struck the woman.

The look of surprise on the man's face was almost comical. As he had turned, Chilcot had worked out the ethics of the case to his own satisfaction. He had all his life followed the rattlesnake code, scorning to shoot a man unawares or without giving the other fellow chance to defend himself. In the present situation, as far as Chilcot could figure it, these men had already drawn their weapons and made their aggressive intentions plain. It was enough that he and they were facing each other and that they could see his own gun. They had brought this down upon their own selves.

Without waiting to aim too perfectly, Chilcot shot the first man in the chest. Then, before the other two had recovered from their shock at this unexpected reversal of fortune, he dropped to the floor and as he did so, fired twice at another of the men, hitting him with both shots. Chilcot rolled to one side, just in case the third man was drawing down on him, but that wasn't at all what was happening. Seeing his two partners killed had been enough for the man. He had turned and run off, racing through the carriages and heading back to the front of the train. Chilcot thought of shooting after him, but then decided that he didn't wish to take the chance of killing an innocent person by mistake.

4

The aftermath of the shooting was a lot of fuss and bother, precisely the very things that Brook Chilcot couldn't abide at any price. He saw the man who had run off join his friend, who had been guarding the crew, and watched as they both mounted up and left without further ado. He had half wondered if they would shoot up the train in revenge as they left, but nothing of the sort happened. Maybe, he thought to himself, they were worried that I had a rifle here as well and would shoot them if they didn't make off at top speed. The notion made him chuckle.

Nobody else was apparently able or willing to take charge of things after the shooting and the departure of the robbers and so, with great reluctance, Chilcot undertook that duty too. He noted down the names and addresses of witnesses, directed that the two corpses be carried to the luggage van and then told everybody who had been robbed to come forward and claim their money or belongings. The escaping outlaw hadn't even thought to snatch up the satchel containing the billfolds and jewellery. 'They were rank amateurs,' he remarked to Jake, 'but those kind can be the deadliest of all.' Then he grimaced in pain.

'Are you all right, Mr Chilcot?' inquired the young man. 'You aren't shot, are you?'

''Course I ain't shot!' exclaimed the old man irascibly. 'Those damned fools didn't get off one single shot. No, it's my back. I ricked it when I threw myself down on the floor.'

'You was so fast. I didn't guess what you were going to do. Is that why you did it, so that they couldn't get a bead on you?'

'Why yes,' said Chilcot. 'When you're up to those tricks and men are shooting at you, the last thing you want is to stand in one place for long. That was an old trick of mine at one time, just dropping to the ground without any warning.'

'Did it always work, sir?'

'Well I'm still here now, ain't I? Yes, it worked well enough, though I never looked to engage in such acrobatics at my time of life, nor specially during a trip on a railroad train.'

It was clear to Chilcot that this would all mean some delay when they changed trains. He had spent long enough in law enforcement to know that the arrival of a train with two dead bodies on board — men, moreover, who had died violently — would need slight investigation by a sheriff or some such. He knew that there was no danger of his being taken into custody over the business, but he wanted to avoid fuss and just continue on his way with the boy.

When they arrived at Jacksonville, where he and Jake Pearson were intending to change trains for Grafton's

Peak, it was immediately apparent that they wouldn't be travelling onwards — not that day at least. Only two trains left the depot in Jacksonville for Grafton's Peak each day; one in the morning and another in the late afternoon. If they were able to get things cleared up in a half hour or so they might make it, but Chilcot knew that realistically, there was no chance of that.

What made matters more complicated from Chilcot's point of view was that many of the passengers on the train who were alighting in Jacksonville, especially those who had seen him in action, were determined that the old man should be lionized and his bravery recognized. This was bad enough to a retiring man like Brook Chilcot, but things took a distinct turn for the worse when he found that the woman on whose behalf he had been prompted to intervene was none other than the wife of Jacksonville's mayor. 'That,' he remarked to his young companion, 'is all we need.'

Just as he had suspected, the mayor made more fuss about the whole thing than anybody else. Probably, thought Chilcot cynically, he'll be after making some political capital of the robbery for purposes of his own. Mayor Dale brushed aside the sheriff's suggestion that he should first take a statement from Chilcot and insisted on escorting the old man and the youngster to Jacksonville's most stylish hotel. 'The two of you are staying here as my guests tonight,' he announced. 'It's the least I can do for the men who stood up to those rogues. My wife tells me that it was her plight which caused you to step in. I can't tell you how grateful I am.'

It was arranged that Chilcot and Jake should have dinner at the hotel and that the sheriff would then drop by and take down Chilcot's account of the robbery and shooting. 'Nobody thinks for a moment as you ought to be setting round in the sheriff's office, waiting on his convenience,' said the mayor. 'If certain people took more trouble then the railroads wouldn't be bothered by such unfortunate occurrences and we'll leave it at that. Anyways, he'll drop by and see you after you've eaten. Don't forget, the city's paying. You fellows have what you please.'

After Mayor Dale had departed, Chilcot observed to Jake, 'He's a wordy bastard and no mistake.' Later that evening, as they sat in the grand restaurant, Jake Pearson ventured to ask a question which had been much on his mind since he had read the bit in the local newspaper concerning Chilcot.

'Hope you don't mind me asking, sir, but I'd sure like to know what happened in Grafton's Peak to make you dig up and leave. Folk still talk about you. My father said you were the best man that ever held the job of sheriff in town, but there's others who . . . ' He stopped, suddenly embarrassed.

'Who say I was a no-good drunk,' Chilcot completed the sentence which the youngster had been unable to bring himself to say out loud. 'That what you was goin' to say?'

'I guess. I heard there'd been a heap of shooting and that later on you'd been sacked, but everybody has a different story about it.'

'And now you'd like to hear from the horse's mouth, as they say, is that it?' asked Chilcot. 'How'd you know if I was tellin' you the truth, though? Us old men are right notorious liars, you know.' His eyes twinkled as he said this and for a moment Jake Pearson found himself viewing Brook W. Chilcot like some amiable uncle. Then he recalled the shooting on the train and he shivered.

'Did any of them stories as you heard make mention o' my brother Talbot?'

'I don't think so,' said the boy. 'I heard there was more than one person killed, but that name doesn't seem to ring a bell.'

Chilcot looked longingly towards the bar, the craving for alcohol coming suddenly upon him. He felt almost overpowered by the thought of a glass of rye. Then he remembered that he was responsible for this young fellow and felt ashamed of himself. To take his mind off the idea of liquor, he began talking about that bloody day over twenty years earlier.

You didn't need to be one of those spiritualists to know that the Adams brothers had it in mind to do away with the sheriff of Grafton's Peak. The only real question was not if, but rather when they would make the attempt on his life. Would it be one of them skulking up on a rooftop with a carbine, to take him unawares? There was no sort of defence that he could muster if they wanted to take that road. But in fairness to those boys, they were not the type of men to play the part of the cowardly assassin. Whatever else they were, those Adams brothers lived by the rattlesnake code, just like Chilcot, and when they came after him, it would be preceded by an open challenge.

Mind, that didn't lessen the danger, because there were four of them and only one of him. Chilcot had never bothered with having a deputy, because he didn't altogether trust any other man to do what was right. As long as all the business, whether legal, financial or what have you, was in his own hands, he knew that matters were being dealt with correctly. That wouldn't be the case once he shared the load with some stranger. Which was all well and good, but meant that in a situation like the present one, where he had his tail in a crack, he was dependent only upon his own self for the preservation of his life. He was sitting in his office brooding about these tricky questions the day after arresting Ezra Adams, when the door burst open and in walked his brother Talbot.

'How are ye, you old cowson?' said his brother cheerfully. 'Not got a word of greeting for your big brother?'

Chilcot leapt to his feet and ran to

embrace his brother. 'God almighty, man,' he said. 'It's surely been some good long while since we met. What's to do?'

'Ah, nothing new. I'm still running that damned store.'

'What about law-keeping? You still head of the safety committee or has that town of yours voted in a sheriff yet?'

'Sheriff? What the devil would we need with one o' them? The breed ain't worth spitting on, present company excepted.'

'You want a drink?' asked Chilcot. 'Rye whiskey do you all right?'

'Yeah, go on. I don't drink as much as once I used to, but a little drop of whiskey'll do me no harm.'

Once their glasses were filled, the two brothers sat down facing each other across the sheriff's desk. Talbot said, 'I hear where your life expectancy is falling daily. I was in the Golden Eagle and it's the theme of general conversation. Folk there are making wagers on how much longer you have to live.'

'Ah that,' said Brook Chilcot dismissively. 'That's a lot of nonsense. I'm surprised at you, Talbot, for taking heed of what some drunk tells you in a barroom.'

'So there's nothing in this story I hear, where these four brothers have sworn an oath to kill you before the month is out?'

'Oh, that. Well, I don't say that it might not be so, but I can handle those boys. Never mind about me; how's that wife of yours? And your boys?'

Talbot waved his hand dismissively at these inquiries. 'They're all robust, thank you. But seriously, what are we going to do about this business?'

'There's no 'we' in the case. This ain't some little hick township like that spot where you've set down your roots. We don't have a vigilance committee here and there's no lynching or aught of that sort.'

'Vigilance committee?' said Talbot, seemingly affronted. 'I ain't head o' no vigilance committee. We don't have any vigilantes nor anything like 'em. Our safety committee's a horse of another colour. Just does what you'd think; keeps things safe for decent folk.'

For a minute or two, neither of the brothers spoke and then Brook said, 'It surely does my heart good to see you again. Let's forget all this and go have something to eat.'

'Suits me well enough, little brother. Then we'll figure out how best to tackle that little problem o' yours.'

They might have backed down from a confrontation in the saloon while Sheriff Chilcot was actually present, but that didn't mean that the Adams brothers were going to behave like Sunday School teachers when Chilcot was out of sight. While Brook and Talbot were catching up on old times, Moses Adams was by himself in the Golden Eagle. He had ordered a few drinks and had neither proffered, nor been asked for, the money for them. He wasn't drunk, but then again neither was he completely sober when the sheriff entered with a man who looked to be about the same age.

There was nothing about the appearance of the man who stepped into the saloon with Sheriff Chilcot to suggest that anybody needed to be at all careful around him. He was aged about forty-five or fifty and was definitely running to fat a little. In addition to that, he had a good-natured face, with twinkling eyes and a nose whose slightly reddened colour suggested that here was a fellow who was probably fonder of the inside of a saloon than the outside. There was certainly no reason for a tough young man like Moses Adams to think that this was anybody deserving of any special respect.

Moses was feeling grieved about having been seen in the street just a couple of days ago with the sheriff pointing a gun at him, which might account for what happened next. When Chilcot and his companion came up to the bar, where Moses Adams was supping a glass of porter, he said to

Sheriff Chilcot, 'You're brave enough when you got the drop on me with a scattergun. You want to try your luck right now, just the two of us outside, man to man?'

Chilcot smiled easily, saying, 'Don't be a damned fool, Adams. I'm sheriff, I ain't about to brawl with you in public.'

'Yellow, hey?'

The sheriff shook his head in amusement and carried on by, but his brother Talbot stopped dead and stared at the young man. Adams said, 'What for you starin' at me? You lookin' for trouble?'

'No,' said Talbot, 'I wouldn't say as I am. Tell you what, though, if you're looking for trouble, I got plenty and to spare.'

The sheriff turned back and said, 'Talbot, no!' His brother took no notice.

'You one of these Adams brothers that I hear so much about?' asked Talbot Chilcot curiously.

'Yeah, that'd be about right. Why,

what d'you hear?'

'Heard you're a bunch of no-count little boys whose ma was a low woman and who never knew who their pa was,' said Talbot in a conversational tone and then, before the other man had quite realized what had been said, the sheriff's brother pulled the pistol from the holster at his hip and smashed it as hard as he could into the side of Moses Adams's head. When the man did not at once fall to the sawdust-strewn floor, Talbot repeated the process twice. Then he leaned over the prone figure and spat on him, saying, 'Next time you're rude to any o' my kin, I'll shoot you down like the mangy dog that you are.'

Brook Chilcot was as taken aback to see this as everybody else in the barroom, although the Lord knew he had a better idea than anybody in the world what a short temper his brother had. He grabbed Talbot's arm and hustled him along to another spot along the bar, saying in a low voice, 'Cris'sake

Talbot, what ails you? There was no call for that.'

'Sure there was,' said his brother imperturbably. 'You was kiddin' me that there wasn't any problem with those boys. Going to leave me out o' the reckoning and just deal with those four men all by your own self. Well now you can't. They got to know that you and me come as a set and that if they want to take you down, then they'll have to try their luck with me as well.'

There was a horrible logic about what his brother said and Brook didn't know whether to be vexed with Talbot or enormously grateful. There was certainly no question now of him facing the Adams brothers alone. By his actions, his brother had, as he had said, made it plain to Ike and the rest that if there was to be any shooting or killing, then they would have to factor Talbot Chilcot into the equation.

'You are one crazy bastard, Talbot, you know that? I can handle this by my own self. It's what they pay me for in this town. We don't run things the way you do. Everything here's done by the rule-book.'

'Piss on that,' said Talbot coarsely. 'No rule-book'll help you when four men come after you. Think any of the men round here will come runnin' to your aid? They won't, I can tell you that for nothing.'

Brook Chilcot didn't say anything; he was thinking about his brother. Talbot had assumed leadership of the vigilance committee in the little place he lived. As a direct consequence of Talbot's ruthless way with those of whose behaviour he disapproved, that town was so safe that a woman and child could walk down the street at any hour of the day or night without fear of being molested or even seeing anything unfitting. Unusually these days, there was still no official lawman in that town. The citizens were so satisfied with the way that Talbot Chilcot and his safety committee kept things running smoothly, that they begged him to continue in the same way, year after year.

'What are you thinking of?' asked Talbot.

'You, you idiot,' said his brother fondly. 'You're right, of course, but I wouldn't want to see you get hurt in a quarrel as is none o' your making.'

'Man's discourteous to my kin, that makes it my business. Are we to expect that fellow's three brothers here this evening? We need to prepare for trouble right now?'

'No, they're out of town on some villainy or other. Heard they gone on the scout in the territories. Doubt they'll be back 'til tomorrow at earliest. I don't rightly know why Moses didn't ride with 'em this time.'

'Gives us time to lay our plans. You know I'm right. You either goin' to let those boys throw their weight around here or you're going to stop 'em. Only way to do that is with a bullet or two. You need my help, baby brother.'

Jake Pearson had listened with bated

breath to the story of things that had happened in his home town years before he was born or thought of. It was as good as a play and he couldn't wait to hear what had happened next. But Mr Chilcot took out his watch and after consulting it, declared, 'Time you was in bed, young Jake.'

'Oh, please sir, not right now. I truly wouldn't be able to sleep, not until I know what happened next. How did it all pan out?'

Chilcot could barely restrain a smile. He had told the story so often over the last few years to audiences in saloons who paid him in bought drinks for hearing a first-hand account of the great Grafton's Peak shootout, but it was refreshing to see this eager, bright-eyed lad who had seemingly never heard the tale. He looked at the watch once again and said, 'Well now, if I tell you how it all turned out, will you promise me to go straight off to bed? You won't be so fired up by all the excitement of the thing that you won't be able to sleep or nothing like that?'

'No sir, I promise straight. Just tell me what happened next and I'll get to my bed without any trouble.'

'Well, it happened like this . . . '

5

When they had left the Golden Eagle after a couple of drinks, Moses Adams was still out cold; lying prostrate on the floor. Nobody was disposed to move him or look as though they had any interest at all in his welfare. Those patrons who had witnessed the way in which Talbot Chilcot had dealt with the man, did not wish to be thought of as associating themselves in any way with his victim; that might not be a healthy move.

As the two brothers strolled to the sheriff's little house on the edge of town, Talbot said, 'How do' you think those boys will play it?'

'I think that they'll come after the both of us with all guns blazing, just as soon as they get back from the Indian Nations. They ain't none of 'em got what you might call a lot of subtlety.

They will come looking for us and hope to outgun us.'

'Yeah,' said Talbot, 'that's how I figured the play too. We used to have some boys like that, living near our town. Odd times, they would come into town and cut up a little rough. 'Till we kind of discouraged them, that is. Some o' them was mighty direct and uncomplicated in their approach as well.'

'Well, we got time to sleep on it. I want to hear what all you been up to lately.'

The next morning, Brook Chilcot woke right early. It was a beautiful day and outside his window he could hear the birds warbling their greetings to the sun. It was a good day to be alive.

Chilcot had neither a wife nor housekeeper to look after his home. He preferred it that way; being responsible for seeing to his own affairs. He cooked breakfast and was about to take a tray upstairs for Talbot, when his brother walked into the kitchen. 'That surely smells good, boy!' exclaimed Talbot, settling himself down at the kitchen table. The two of them demolished between them a loaf of bread, a half-dozen eggs, a plate of bacon and a pot of coffee. Talbot lit his pipe and said, 'Well then, what's to do today?'

'You mean about the Adams boys?'

'No, I meant about your roses. Of course about the Adams boys, you lunkhead.'

'I don't know if they'll be back in town today. If so, it won't be 'til evening, I reckon.'

'I suppose we can't ride out to their place and brace 'em there? You say they live in some old farmhouse?'

'I'd sooner give 'em the chance to do nothing. I don't want to go a-huntin' them down. If they come looking for me, well that's another thing altogether.'

'Happen you're right,' conceded Talbot. 'So how do we play it?'

'I guess the first move would be to make sure we don't get caught with our pants down. Let's get to the office and make sure as we're properly dressed for the occasion.'

As they walked into town, Talbot said, 'So what is it with this place?'

'What do you mean?'

'You only got to look around to see that there's money here and folk are doing well. But I don't see no mines, logging camps, manufacturing or aught else. Where's the money comin' from?'

'Hypocrisy,' said Brook shortly. 'This town grows rich on it and I'm part of the whole game.'

'How so?'

'You don't see where the money comes from, because it all takes place under counters, in dark corners and behind closed doors. You notice how many rough-looking characters you see about here? Mexicans, breeds, low white men and all sorts of others?'

'Surely. They don't look to be causing trouble, though.'

''Course not, that'd be killing the goose that laid the golden eggs. You name a racket and it flourishes right

87

here in Grafton's Peak. Running guns into the Indian Nations, smuggling liquor and tobacco down into Mexico, buying and selling bullion that comes from the Lord knows where; this town is the centre of it all.'

They had arrived at the sheriff's office by now and Brook took out a key and opened the door. Once they were inside, he raked out the stove and laid a new fire and got it going. Then he set the coffee pot atop of the stove and went over to the closet where he kept his weapons. Talbot said, 'How come you put up with all of it? You're supposed to be the sheriff, ain't you?'

'Sure I'm sheriff. But the town council here's more worried about me assessing taxes and collecting 'em than they are about trade in illegal rifles or smuggling moonshine to the red man. Long as the town is peaceful and quiet and there's no shooting on the streets, that's about enough for 'em. You might say as my job is to keep things tucked out of sight. I don't go inquiring too closely into much of the commerce in Grafton's Peak, but I make damned sure that a lone woman can walk down Main Street after dark without being bothered none. That's all anybody wants. I tell you now, nobody goin' to thank me for starting some sort of range war with the Adams boys. Standing up to them was by way of being my own idea.'

Brook brought out of the closet various powder flasks, boxes of balls, ramrods, copper caps and various other items relating to the maintenance and loading of firearms. He turned to his brother and said, 'What do you favour, Talbot? I've got a couple of sawn-offs here, rifles, what have you.'

'Reach me over one o' them scatter-guns.'

Brook handed his brother the weapon that he had used a day or two earlier in his confrontation with the Adams brothers. He said, 'This one's ready loaded. It's double charged and full of various bits of metal. It's a regular blunderbuss.'

'Got a sling for it? I wouldn't mind having this and a rifle too. Those fellows sound like they're apt to be handy with guns. Need to make sure that we don't have to start fooling around with a powder flask while they're raining lead on us.' As he attached the sling to the shortened scattergun, Talbot said, 'So are you saying that the town would put up with having some rogues lean on the local saloon, because there's so much profit riding on other matters, things that tend towards making everybody well off?'

Brook shrugged a little uncomfortably. 'Folk round here know how to turn a blind eye sometimes.'

'You got a little fat to wipe round the mouth o' the chambers?' asked Talbot. He continued, 'You've changed, Brook. Not so long since, you would o' scorned to be a part of such crookedness. You wouldn't o' let things get this far before cracking down hard on those four brothers. You know it's true.'

'It could be so, but then I ain't as young as once I was. I like a quiet life these days. Collecting taxes and filling in forms suits me just fine now. Anyways, I decided to put a stop to those boys' carryings-on before you even fetched up here. I got my limits, same as everybody.'

After a cup of coffee, the sheriff thought that it might be prudent for them to have a stroll round the town, maybe visit the depot and so on, to get some feel for what might be happening. Brook Chilcot carried a rifle under his arm, which was a novel sight in Grafton's Peak, while the man at his side carried not only a rifle, but also had a shotgun slung over his shoulder. The less reputable men on the streets that day watched uneasily at the sight of Sheriff Chilcot roaming the town, seemingly looking for trouble. Some had heard about the stranger knocking down Moses Adams yesterday although nobody was sure who this fellow was.

There were those who guessed that Chilcot might at last have decided to engage a deputy. If so, it was funny that he hadn't gone for a local man.

As they came to the depot, there was a furtive hissing from between two buildings and when he turned to find the source of the noise, Sheriff Chilcot saw that it was one of his regular informants; a mean-looking drunk called Cahill. 'Come hither, Sheriff,' said Cahill softly. 'I got somethin' to tell you.'

'Wait here,' said Brook to his brother. 'This fellow sometimes has useful gossip. I'll be back directly.' He walked over casually to where the unkempt and down-at-heel figure of Joe Cahill lurked in the shadows like some nocturnal beast caught out in the open after the sun had risen. 'Well,' said the sheriff, 'how's it going, Joe?'

'Awful hard, Sheriff. A fellow can't find two dimes to rub together these days. What with that dad-burned recession and all that they talk of in the newspapers.'

'Why yes,' said Chilcot gravely, 'I do hear where the recession has proved to be pretty grim for a lot of honest tradesmen such as yourself. What can we do for each other?'

'It's about those four boys as you got crosswise to.'

'The Adams brothers? Yes, what have you heard?'

'That they're a-planning for to kill you.'

Chilcot laughed. 'If you think that's worth anything to me, then you best had think again. Everybody in town's sayin' the self-same thing.'

'Yeah, but not everyone knows when they due to do it,' said Cahill, giving the sheriff a sly, sidelong glance. 'I'd o' said that was worth something.'

'Happen it may be,' said Chilcot. 'All right, when did you say they're coming?'

'I didn't. Yet.'

Sheriff Chilcot sighed and withdrew a couple of bills from his pocket. He had what he privately referred to as his 'skunk fund'; a sum of cash set aside for paying men like Cahill. In his accounts, this was disguised as 'sundry expenditure'.

'Twenty is all I can let you have, Joe. Mind, if it turns out to be a true bill, I don't say as we might not be able to find you a little more.'

Joe Cahill snatched greedily at the proffered money. He said, 'Moses wired his brothers, sent a message to reach them at the junction. They're that mad, from what I heard, that they goin' to leave they horses there and just hop on the train this very morning. They're in that much of a hurry to kill you, Sheriff. Should get here a little after one, if they caught the morning train.'

Rejoining his brother, Chilcot said, 'We've got three hours to lay our plans, if what I just heard is true.'

Back at the office, Talbot came up with what seemed to him like a right smart idea. 'How'd it be,' he said, 'if we rode on ahead down the railroad track and stopped that train 'fore it reaches Grafton's Peak? That way, we can settle it all without anybody in the town being set at hazard?'

'And then later have folk whispering that we acted like a couple of bush-whackers? No, I want anything I do to be in front of the town. 'Sides which, I don't despair of making those boys see sense. All I ask is that they stop their tricks in town. I don't much care what they get up to elsewhere.'

'You're dreaming. It'll come to shooting, you see if I'm not right.'

Slowly, the hours wore by. The Chilcot brothers checked and re-checked their weapons, oiled them, made coffee and then checked their guns one last time. In between times, they talked in a desultory way of their childhood memories and about Talbot's present family life. Brook wondered if anybody else had heard that the Adams brothers were coming in on the next train from the junction. Most likely they had; the fellow running the telegraph office wasn't the most discreet of individuals. He just hoped that most people would have the sense to keep away from the depot and not go flocking there, like they were coming to watch a carnival sideshow.

At a quarter after twelve, Brook said, 'Let's be getting down to the station. It ain't often the case, but odd times, that train has been a mite early. I want that we should be sure to meet it today.'

The depot didn't seem to Sheriff Chilcot any more crowded than usual, which gave him to hope that word had not spread about the coming confrontation. That was good, because if it came to fighting, he didn't want to be worrying about a crowd of civilians getting caught in the crossfire.

It was, after all, a good thing that they had got to the station early, because about twenty before one, the mournful whistle of the approaching train could be heard as it puffed its way towards Grafton's Peak. It looked like it would only be another ten minutes or so before Sheriff Chilcot and his brother would know how the cards were going to fall.

Brook Chilcot had quite understood that he and his brother would speak to the men as they alighted from the train and then, after having set the case out fairly, would see which way Ike Adams and his brothers wanted to take it. The sheriff of Grafton's Peak was a man who always liked to know how things would be, in as far as that was possible. So it was, that he was far from pleased when his brother Talbot said casually, 'I'm going up onto that water tower, so's I can give you flanking fire if needed.' Without waiting for an answer, Talbot went sprinting across to the ladder leading up to the little tower.

'No, that wasn't what we agreed . . . ' began Brook, before it occurred to him that this was what his brother had perhaps planned to do all along. It made perfect sense; to have one of them high up and out of sight, covering the other. But there was no time to fret further about it now, because the train was drawing into the depot and in another minute or two, Chilcot knew that he might be fighting for his life.

There weren't more than a handful of folk getting off the train at Grafton's Peak. A couple of fellows that looked like commercial travellers, a family that had been on a vacation somewhere, and then, just when he thought he'd been sold a pup by Joe Cahill, the sheriff saw three men stepping down from the rear coach. Sure enough, it was Ike, Jethro and Ezra. Chilcot had already begun to walk towards the three men, when Ike turned and handed down a woman from the same coach that he had lately left. She was exceedingly dark-skinned and Chilcot wondered if this was the squaw that Ike Adams was rumoured to be shacked up with at odd times in the territories. To his amazement, there was a child with the woman; a little boy of maybe ten or eleven years of age.

A sudden doubt assailed Sheriff

Chilcot. Surely to God even a scoundrel like Ike Adams wouldn't be after bringing his wife and child to a killing? Then Ike caught a sight of the sheriff and said something to his brothers, who both turned to face Chilcot. For a second, the three outlaws faced the sheriff at a distance of thirty yards or so, nobody moving and none of them seeming to know what to do next. Then Ike called above the hissing of the locomotive, 'What say we call a truce, Chilcot? I brought my family back with me. You'll not be seeing any of us in town all that much from here on in.'

Relief washed through Brook Chilcot and for a moment or two, he half persuaded himself that this was all square and that Ike Adams and his brothers were backing down. Then he recollected himself and thought about who he was dealing with. He kept hold of the rifle that he was carrying tucked under his arm and shouted back, 'You ain't a-comin' after me for vengeance, Ike? That's what I heard.'

'You ever hear of a man bringing his child to a gunfight?' asked Adams rhetorically, waving his hand and indicating the woman and child who stood a few feet away.

This was a good point and if Brook Chilcot had been taking his stand alone at the depot that day, there's no telling how things might have gone. But Talbot was something else again and he'd been ruling his own town with gun and rope for so long that he hardly ever believed in the good intentions of anybody; even his most intimate friends. It was Talbot, perched up in the water tower, who precipitated the chain of bloody events which engulfed them all before the train had even finished taking on water.

Now both Brook and Talbot Chilcot had been so preoccupied with thinking about the return to town of Ike, Jethro and Ezra, that they had more or less forgotten about Moses; out of the four brothers, the one with most reason to be pursuing a vendetta. While the sheriff stood there, his rifle still pointing at the ground, Ike Adams raised his hands in a pacifying gesture, saying, 'Come on, man, things are gettin' out of hand here.'

Just as Ike's hands moved, Talbot shouted down a warning. 'Brook, it's a trap! There's one of 'em coming up behind you.'

Chilcot snatched a look behind and sure enough, he saw Moses Adams hurrying towards him. Then his brother shouted again. 'Look out!' This was followed almost immediately by the crack of a rifle shot, which echoed across the depot. A woman screamed and the sheriff saw that both Jethro and Ezra were pulling their pistols. Ike was down, presumably taken by a shot from Talbot. There was more screaming and out of the corner of his eye, Chilcot could see men and women running for cover. He raised his rifle and shot Ezra. Then he threw himself to the ground and rolled towards the wheels of the train. A bullet smacked into the woodwork of the carriage, no more than a foot above his head. There was the dull boom of a scattergun and then another shot came towards the sheriff. He looked across towards the ticket office and saw that Moses was drawing down on him. Sheriff Chilcot went for his own pistol, but knew that he wouldn't be able to reach it in time. There was another roar and Moses was knocked to the ground by the blast of Talbot's scattergun. His brother had evidently descended from his perch and come up behind the other man.

Chilcot jumped up and then went jinking across the open space, his eyes casting around for anybody on his feet and with a gun in his hand. There didn't seem to be any targets left and so he stopped and surveyed the scene more carefully.

All four of the Adams brothers lay dead. There were no other casualties that the sheriff could see. He looked round slowly, pleased to be alive but at the same time puzzled as to how things had turned sour so fast. He had little time to stop and think about this, though, because a young boy came hurtling at him like a wild animal. He had a glimpse of black hair and then the kid was grabbing and kicking at Chilcot, screaming at the top of his voice, 'You killed my pa. I'll shoot you, you'll see. I'm goin' to kill you as well.' He tried to ward the child off without hurting him.

The Indian woman that he'd seen Ike Adams helping down from the train came up and restrained the boy, enfolding him in her arms. Chilcot tried to frame some words, an apology perhaps for killing the father of her child. He opened his mouth to speak and the woman spat in his face and turned away, taking her son with her. He heard her say, 'Come Keith. You must be the man now.' Even at the time, it struck him as a very strange thing to say to a child of that age, given the circumstances.

Sheriff Chilcot stood there as some of those who had sought shelter came out to see who had been killed. The area between the train and the water tower looked like a slaughterhouse. Moses, the nearest of the corpses, had had half his head blown away by the scattergun which Talbot had wielded to such deadly effect. At that moment, his brother came striding up; a look of satisfaction on his face. He said, 'Lord, baby brother, you didn't get but one of 'em. Strikes me as you're losing your grip. I don't know what would o' befell you had I not been here to cover your back.'

'What the hell happened?' asked Chilcot, looking around in despair. 'I thought everything was going to fizzle out.'

'Not a bit of it. I saw that bastard over yonder, the one as had his woman with him. I seed him goin' for his gun. Same time as I saw that other fellow coming after you from behind. Him I knocked down in the saloon.'

A horrible feeling began to creep into Chilcot's heart. He said, 'Talbot, Ike

Adams wasn't going for his gun. He was just showing his open hands, as much to say, 'Let's leave this be.' I don't believe he was after shooting me. As for Moses . . . ' He thought hard. Had Moses really been coming on to attack him? Or had he rather been coming to meet his brothers and then been surprised to find the sheriff there with a rifle in his hand? Was the whole thing some ghastly mistake?

It was plain that Talbot was afflicted with no such misgivings. To him, the case was simple and straightforward as could be. He had seen his brother being menaced by four outlaws and had saved his life by shooting first. Chilcot shook his head, overwhelmed by the magnitude of what had happened. All he could think of was that poor boy, orphaned by what might be a stupid error on the part of a trigger-happy vigilante who always shot first and then picked over the bones later to see if the killing had been justified. He loved his brother dearly, as God knew, but he was

105

under no illusions whatsoever about the type of man he was. Chilcot turned to his brother and said, 'Talbot, I need some time alone.'

6

'And that's how it was, all those years ago,' said Chilcot. He looked at his watch and said, 'Lord almighty, boy, you needs must be gettin' to bed this very second. Just look at the time!'

'But what I don't make out — ' began Jake Pearson, but the old man cut in rapidly.

'Never you mind what you do or don't make out. We had us a deal. It's surely time you was tucked up asleep. Come on now.'

'Will you tell me the rest tomorrow, sir?'

'There ain't a whole heap more to tell, but yes, such as there is, I'll give you chapter and verse when we're both safe on the train to Grafton's Peak.'

After he had got the youngster safely to bed, Chilcot returned to the dining room, where he sat for a while drinking a glass of juice. The manager pressed him to accept a bottle of champagne, with the mayor's compliments, but he declined firmly. He wasn't about to drink anything in the alcoholic line until he had delivered that boy back to his folks.

As he sat there, Brook Chilcot mulled over what he had told young Jake about the shootout at the depot in Grafton's Peak. Shootout? Hell, it was more like a massacre. To this very day, Chilcot did not know whether his brother Talbot had saved his life by a timely display of marksmanship or whether he had lost Brook his job and sent him on a downward spiral which had ended in his being a lonely old man who spent his life cadging drinks in saloons. It was a regular conundrum to which he never had figured out the answer. And now that little boy who had told Chilcot that he would shoot him was the sheriff of Grafton's Peak! It just went to show that you never could tell how life would turn out.

Would anybody in the town recall him after all this time? wondered the former sheriff of Grafton's Peak. Maybe one or two might, but his appearance had surely changed since those days. For one thing, his hair had been lustrous and dark at that time. Now it was sparse and white. Chances were that nobody would connect the shaky old man that he had since become with that tough and indomitable man who had once been their sheriff.

Up in his bed, Jake Pearson was quite unable to sleep. The story of that gun battle at the depot had passed into legend and his father, who had been no older than Jake was now, had witnessed the whole thing. But hearing about a shootout like that from people who had merely seen what took place was a mighty different thing from being told the truth of the matter by the man who was at the centre of it all.

From the little that old Mr Chilcot had let slip when first they met, Jake supposed that the little boy at the depot that day must be the present sheriff of Grafton's Peak. He pictured Keith Tranter as he knew him and found it all but impossible to see him in the role of a frightened little boy. Fact was, he had always found Sheriff Tranter a pleasant and agreeable fellow.

Before he drifted off to sleep, Jake fell to wondering what his mother would have to say when he turned up tomorrow in the company of the old man. She'd most likely go plumb crazy. Then again, his ma was always keenly aware of what was fitting and decent. Jake thought that she would not be able to express her honest views and opinions on his truancy while there was company in the house. Also, Mr Chilcot had hinted that he would try his best to smooth things over with Jake's ma and he struck one most powerful as a fellow who kept his word. Heck, it probably wouldn't be that bad and whatever happened the next day, his adventure had been worth any scolding that he might receive.

The following day was the very embodiment of all Chilcot's worst fears. Mayor Dale and his wife turned up at the hotel to see them safely to the station and on to the train to Grafton's Peak. Worse still was where the mayor was accompanied by a newspaper reporter, which confirmed what Chilcot had all along suspected, which was that Dale was making some capital of this whole affair for his own purposes.

The young man from the paper, who to Chilcot's eyes looked as though he could not be long out of school, showed an alarming curiosity about every aspect of the business.

'Is it true, sir, that you were once sheriff of Grafton's Peak?'

'Oh, that was years ago,' replied Chilcot dismissively. 'I can't think that anybody would be interested in all that now.'

'It's the human angle, sir. Don't like to contradict you, but that's just precisely what our readers do like to see. Wasn't there some sort of fight up that way, before you left the town?'

'It could be so. It was all so long ago.'

While the impudent young cub was doing his best to pump Chilcot, the local sheriff showed up with a statement for Chilcot to sign. It accorded roughly with the facts and so after glancing at it, the old man scrawled his name at the bottom and the party set off for the depot, where Mayor Dale had arranged another little surprise for them. To Chilcot's amazement and horror, a platform had been set up on the open ground in front of the station and standing next to it, a trio consisting of a concertina player, violinist and a fellow with a fife were giving a spirited rendition of various patriotic tunes. Chilcot turned to the boy at his side and said softly, 'There's an election in the wind or I'm a Dutchman. That mayor is milking this for all it's worth.'

'Ain't you pleased though, sir?' asked the boy.

'Do I look like the sort of damned fool who's likely to be impressed by somebody playing *Yankee Doodle Dandy* on a tin whistle?' asked Chilcot rhetorically.

Before the train left, Mayor Dale gave a little speech, thanking Chilcot for rescuing his wife and all the other passengers on the train. He then promised that if and when he was re-elected, he would use every endeavour to ensure that railroad trains running through what would soon become the territory of Oklahoma were made safe for all decent folks. There was only a small crowd of loafers and people waiting for the train to hear this pretty little speech, but Chilcot supposed that every little helped when you were fighting to maintain your position in the town.

To crown it all, as Chilcot and his young friend were being ushered on to the train, a little girl was waved forward to present them with a bouquet of flowers from the grateful citizenry.

Once they were safely settled on the train and it had pulled out of the station, Chilcot took the bunch of flowers and walked down the coach until he found a lonely-looking, middle-aged woman. 'Excuse me, ma'am,' he said, 'I was wondering if you would accept these flowers? I'm sure that they would grace your home better than they would mine.' It was a meaningless piece of fluff, but the woman smiled gratefully at Chilcot and took the flowers. Back in his seat, he said to Jake Pearson, 'I don't know what kind of fool I would have looked stepping off the train, waving a bunch of damned roses!'

Young Jake was obviously not all that interested in how Chilcot had rid himself of the flowers. Since he had got up that day, it had been quite strikingly clear that all he was waiting for was to hear about the aftermath of the shooting at Grafton's Peak railroad station. Chilcot knew this very well, but it was amusing him to watch the youngster wriggling like a kid who wanted to know how an exciting bedtime story ended.

It took all of five minutes before the boy could no longer hold it in and asked outright. 'Sir, you said last night as you would tell the rest of your tale. Touching upon what happened after those men were all shot.'

'Did I? I don't recollect saying nothing to that end.' Then, seeing the boy's face fall, Chilcot chuckled and said, 'I don't know that anything much happened afterwards, other than everybody in town turning against me and me losing my position as sheriff.'

'How so? I'd o' thought they would've been right glad to see the end of those men as had been troubling them.'

'Well now, you see, to understand that, you have to know that most everybody in Grafton's Peak at that time was getting some kind of advantage from all the traffic passing through the town in bullion, guns and I don't know what all else. Nobody much minded what was happening outside the town boundary. As long as things were quiet in Grafton's Peak itself, they were content to turn a blind eye to all sorts of things.'

'Only I guess things weren't really quiet after that big gun battle?'

'Well, there was that. The other thing was that folk said that me and my brother had gunned those boys down needlessly. It was said that we'd decided to kill them and then just set out and murdered the four of them.'

Jake looked puzzled at this. He said, 'But those men had sworn vengeance against you, hadn't they? Weren't they coming after you, for to kill you?'

'I thought so then, but now? I tell you, boy, I don't know if I did the right thing that day and that's the God's honest truth. I only had Joe Cahill's word for that and he vanished soon after. Just dug up and left town. Then again, why would Ike Adams have fetched his wife and child with him on that train, if he was planning on starting a shooting match with me as soon as he hit town?'

'You mean he might not o' been going for his gun when your brother shot him?'

'Oh, that? No, Ike wasn't going for his gun at that point. He just turned his palms outwards, showing me he wasn't after trouble. Talbot saw his hands twitch and that was enough for him.'

The young man sitting opposite Chilcot appeared to be genuinely disturbed at the idea that his new friend might really have been party to the killing of four men without any need. He said, 'What about the other one, though? Him as was coming up behind you?'

'Moses? I suppose he might have been fixin' to bash me over the head or some such. I doubt he meant to kill me, though. No, Talbot was in the habit of shooting men at the slightest excuse. It was what had kept his own town so safe and secure for decent people for so long and he couldn't see why the same tactic wouldn't answer in Grafton's Peak. My brother, God rest him, didn't set a whole store by human life. He had the soul of a vigilante. It was what he was good at.'

They neither of them spoke for a minute or two. Chilcot had in some slight way enjoyed basking in the admiration of this pleasant young man and now the youth looked disappointed, as though he had discovered that his idol had feet of clay. At length, Jake said, 'It ain't exactly how I thought it would be . . . '

Chilcot cut in sharply, saying in a rough voice, 'What, you thought this was like some story-book adventure, where the fearless sheriff defeats a dozen men and saves the young lady who's tied up in their lair? Life's not like that, son. It's nine times out of ten a muddle and confusion, and you don't know 'till years later if you did right or wrong.' He spoke perhaps more sharply than he intended, feeling a little vexed at seeing the new way that the boy looked at him; like he was just another adult who got things wrong. Chilcot added more gently, 'It's oft-times the way. A man does what he thinks is the right thing and then he finds he's been a mite too hasty and what he did wasn't the best as he could o' done. It's an old story. It's a fearful thing to take a man's life and if it consoles you any, my life didn't quite prosper after that particular killing.'

'You lose your job?'

'Eventually. Nobody cared overmuch about the death of the Adams brothers. Truth to tell, most folk in Grafton's Peak was glad to see the back of 'em.'

'So how come they didn't want you as sheriff any more?'

''Cause o' what happened next. Or rather, what didn't happen next.'

'I don't understand.'

'It's like this,' said Chilcot, 'you 'member how I told you that a lot of the town relied upon those shiftless and suspicious characters who used to make Grafton's Peak their base for various things that they got up to far away from the town? Well, after me and Talbot killed the Adams brothers, there were bits in various newspapers about how vigilantes now ruled the roost in that town. Talbot was tolerable well known as being a man who ran his own town by killing those who caused trouble there. The hint was that now Grafton's Peak was goin' to be run under the same system, with suspects just shot down without trial.'

'Didn't you try to explain what had happened?'

'No point. Enough people saw it for themselves. Saw that poor boy orphaned in front of their eyes. But that was nothing; they might have forgiven me for that. The chief thing as happened was that all those who had been carrying on their various illicit businesses and using the town as a safe haven, they all decided that if there was going to be vigilante rule, then Grafton's Peak wasn't the place for them any longer. Trade fell off overnight. All the Mexicans, the men bringing bullion through from the south, the others who were ferrying liquor to Mexico, they all moved their business elsewhere. None of 'em wanted to run the risk of being the next victims of the vigilantes who the papers told them were running Grafton's Peak now.'

'That boy, the one who said he was going to kill you. You think that he's Sheriff Tranter?'

'Well Tranter was the name of Ike Adam's squaw and her son was called Keith, so I guess so. Maybe he ain't so very like his pa. I certainly hope so for the sake of your town. It's a terrible thing when a bad sheriff is in charge.'

The rest of the journey was a little subdued, with young Jake looking thoughtful and not inclined towards further conversation. This suited Chilcot well enough and the two of them just sat there, staring from the window for most of the time until the train gave a whistle and began drawing into the depot at Grafton's Peak.

The former sheriff of Grafton's Peak looked about him with frank and undisguised curiosity. He had not been here for well over twenty years and wondered how the place had changed since his departure. The first impression was of prosperity and stability; this was a place which was doing very well for itself. You could see at once that there was money here; there was none of that tired and rundown feel about the town that you found as soon as you set foot out of the train at many other little places.

'What do you think of it?' asked Jake Pearson.

'I think it looks just fine, son. It's certainly on the up since I was myself last in these here parts.'

As they walked towards the store which Jake Pearson's mother owned and ran, and where he thought she'd be most likely to be found at that time of day, Chilcot pondered the fact that he had evidently fallen in the youngster's estimation since admitting that he had probably shot all those men needlessly. I should've kept my own counsel and let him carry on thinking me a fine fellow, he thought to himself. Then he was suddenly disgusted. Hero worship ain't worth much if it's based upon a lie, he told himself. The sooner that boy learns that real life is a lot different from what you might find in a penny dreadful, the better.

Pearson's Hardware Store was a little wooden building, tucked away down a side street. Despite not being in a central location, the business looked to be thriving, with customers coming and going in a steady stream. Before they entered the store, Chilcot halted and said to Jake, 'Wait up, boy. You and me need to have a word or two.'

'What is it, sir?'

'Don't you go a-tellin' your mother about guns or shooting or anything of that nature, you hear what I tell you?' The boy looked uncertain and Chilcot continued, 'I don't want to see your ma distressed because she thinks you're planning to take up arms on her behalf. She'd be frightened to death. You tell her you came to beg my aid. It'll be less of a fear for her.'

The look of respect came back into Jake Pearson's face and he said, 'I surely don't think I could have hoped for anybody who would o' taken better care of me and been so concerned about my ma into the bargain. You been a true friend to me, Mr Chilcot.'

'Well, well, let that be as it will. Just don't go talking about guns is all I suggest.'

When they walked into the store, a dead silence fell; by which Chilcot assumed that it was generally known that the boy had not arrived at school and that he was missing. A woman of perhaps thirty-five years of age gave a single, piercing scream and then hurried round from the counter and ran to the young man, enfolding him in her arms and hugging him fiercely. Then she released him, stepped back a pace and delivered a sharp slap to his face that echoed through the place like a pistol shot. 'Don't you ever dare to pull a stunt like that again, Jacob Pearson,' she said angrily, her eyes glittering with unshed tears. 'I have been plumb distracted.'

Throughout this affecting scene, Chilcot stood back out of sight, hoping that he would be able to take his leave without drawing too much attention to himself. It was not to be, because Mrs Pearson, who had apparently seen him entering with Jake, turned to him and said to her son, 'Who's this, might I ask? He led you astray, maybe? What in the blazes is going on?'

'Ma, don't speak so,' said the boy. 'You got this man to thank for bringing me home again. This is Mr Chilcot and he has looked after me like I might have been his own flesh and blood.'

His mother looked hard at Chilcot and said quietly, 'Has he now?' Without taking her eyes from Chilcot's face, she raised her voice and announced generally to her customers, 'You folk know what a torment this boy has been to me of late. You'll none o' you mind if I tell you as I'm closing up for the day now.' Discreetly, but with many a sidelong glance at the white-haired old man standing unobtrusively in the shadows, everybody moved towards the door and left. Chilcot was in the process of sidling out himself, when Mrs Pearson said, 'Not you, Mr Chilcot. You just stay right where you are, if you please.'

When only Chilcot, Jake and his mother remained in the store, the woman went over and locked the door, turning the sign so that it indicated to those looking in the window that the business was now closed. Having done this, she went over to her son and put her hand on his shoulder, saying, 'I'm sorry for striking you, son, but you'll own if ever a boy deserved it, that boy was you.'

'I guess I asked for it, Ma. I'm sorry.'

Mrs Pearson turned to Chilcot and said, 'I wouldn't have recognized you, Mr Chilcot. You've changed that much.'

Then, feeling perhaps that this was rather a personal remark to make, she continued, 'I didn't mean to say that you looked old or nothing . . . ' She stopped speaking, as though she felt that she might be causing offence.

'Don't you fret about that, ma'am,' said Chilcot cheerfully. 'I certainly changed somewhat since I left this town a while back. You recollect me from them days, seemingly?'

'Recollect Sheriff Chilcot? I should just about say that I do, although I was only a little girl when you left. I suppose you and that wretched son of mine'll tell me now why he didn't go back to school and now turns up with you?'

7

After Chilcot had explained that Jake Pearson had come in search of him after seeing the piece in the newspaper, begging his aid against the men who were putting the bite on Mrs Pearson and that he had at once undertaken to bring the boy home to her, he thought that Mrs Pearson looked a little more kindly towards him.

'I'm obliged to you for bringing him home safe and sound,' she said. 'As for you helping out here, that's nothing to be concerned about. I can handle my own problems without involving others. Jacob had no business going off so to draw somebody else into the matter. Mind, I'm grateful to you, just a little vexed with him is all.'

'Your son meant well. He was worried about you. He might o' gone about things different, maybe, but his heart was set right.'

Mrs Pearson looked fondly across at her son. 'Yes, I know that. He's a good boy.'

'Well then, I guess I'll be getting along,' said Chilcot. 'It was a pleasure meeting you, ma'am.'

'Why, don't be absurd! I couldn't think of you leaving at once. You must at least eat with us and spend one night in town. You can't hardly go rushing off as soon as you've got here.'

It took a little persuasion, but when Chilcot saw that the woman really meant her offer of hospitality, he said, 'That's right nice of you. I won't say as I was really looking forward to travelling straight back again today.'

Back at the Pearsons' house, his mother said to Jake, 'You scoot off up to the spare room now and make up a bed for Mr Chilcot. You know where the bedding's kept.' When her son had gone, she turned to Chilcot and said, 'Truly, I am grateful. I can't think what got into his head.'

'He wanted to find help for you is all. He told me somewhat about your difficulties.'

A careworn and unhappy look passed briefly across the woman's face, like a cloud momentarily obscuring the sun. Then she was her cheerful self again and said, 'Don't you fret none about me. I can handle myself, I reckon.'

Yes, thought Chilcot to himself, I dare say as you can in most things. But this is something you can't handle and, what's more, you know it. He said nothing, though, other than, 'Just as you say, ma'am.'

During the meal, Chilcot was tentative and polite, but at the same time exceedingly firm. He said to Mrs Pearson, 'Ma'am, you've no husband to speak for you, nor any brothers from what your son tells me. I'd count it an honour if you'd just let me represent your interests to those as are causing you this trouble. I'm sure that I can reason with them.'

'You mean serve them as you did

those fellows on the train that my son has told me of? No, it's kind of you, but it's not your affair.'

This sounded final enough, but Chilcot was not about to be brushed off. He smiled and said, 'It would be my pleasure, ma'am, truly. Tell you what, why not give me leave to stay for a day or two and allow me to help out in your store? That way, folk might see that you have what might be called a male protector and will not try to bully you. You know how foolish some people can be about a lone woman.'

Jake's mother looked long and hard at Chilcot for a few seconds, trying to gauge his intentions, and then, to her son's relief, said, 'All right, Mr Chilcot. If you want to come down to the store tomorrow and just kind of hang around, helping me tidy up and suchlike, I don't say that I mightn't find it a comforting thing to have you around. I don't look for any violence, mind.'

Chilcot said laughingly, 'Why, ma'am,

you flatter me! I'm an old man.'

The next day in the hardware store, Mrs Pearson had one of the busiest, if least profitable, mornings that she ever could recall. It seemed that everybody in town wished to visit her and ask about her son's welfare, word having spread that the prodigal had returned. None of these early customers really wanted anything in particular; they only came to express their joy that the boy had turned up safe and sound. Some of those who had been in the shop the day before had caught the name 'Chilcot' and had reported to their friends and neighbours that the famous man himself had been sighted in Pearson's hardware store. This was news indeed and so those first few visitors were also hoping to hear what the former sheriff was doing back in Grafton's Peak and what his connection with Mrs Pearson's boy might be. When those first visitors found that Brook Chilcot was present in person and stacking shelves in the store, they could hardly wait to spread the news far and wide.

Throughout the morning, a steady stream of people entered Mrs Pearson's store. None of them appeared to want anything more than a packet of pins or some similar trifling item, but each stopped to talk at length with the proprietor, while casting long looks at the old man pottering about with a broom or straightening out the stock. This really beat all and not one person could make out what the Sam Hill was going on. They were all of them too well bred to ask a direct question and so left, quite perplexed, to tell their friends that if they wanted to see the wonder of the age, then they best get themselves down to the hardware store this very minute.

The gossip about Mrs Pearson's new help was largely confined to the wives of respectable men in town, most of whom knew the Widow Pearson from church. Such rumours had not yet penetrated the Golden Eagle, though, where, despite it still lacking a few minutes to twelve, three men were sitting at a table supping ale.

'We don't get that damned woman in line this week, things are like to turn hard for us with others,' remarked one of these men to his companions. 'I already heard some cowson jokin' 'bout how that Pearson woman got more balls than the blacksmith or the lumber merchant.'

'You got that right.'

'Well,' said the third, an ill-favoured man in early middle-age with a grim and determined look about him, 'I'd say we've already given her all the slack we can afford. We even lessened the terms for her, but she still won't play. What say we go down there this day to her store and break a few things, show her that the time for foolin' round is long past?'

It has to be said that none of those three men had any liking or respect for women and the fact that it was a woman who was standing up to them sat ill with the whole crew. The idea of making that tough and contemptuous young widow scream a bit and beg them to stop was a pleasing one to them. They all nodded with pleasant anticipation, gulped down their drinks and then stood up to leave. Before they did so, one remarked, 'We best not hurt her, though. Boss said not to do aught of that kind without we clear it with him first.'

* * *

'You ever work in a store before, Mr Chilcot?' asked Jake's mother.

'Can't say as I did, ma'am. Done most everything else in my life, but working like this ain't been one of 'em. I always preferred to be outside in God's great outdoors.'

'Yes, there's something to be said for that. I'd sooner be gardening than standing behind this counter, any day of the week. I really do appreciate you taking the time and trouble to bring my boy back, you do know that?'

'Oh, that's nothing to the purpose,' said Chilcot, a little embarrassed. 'He's a nice kid; I couldn't see him wandering the world without anybody to look after his interests. It was a pleasure to share his company.'

'You know,' said Mrs Pearson, looking at Chilcot searchingly, 'you're not a bit like I would have thought. Not from what was said about you after you . . . left.'

'After I was kicked out you mean? I dare say I deserved some of what was said about me.'

'I was little more than a child, but they painted you as some bloodthirsty killer who wanted to take over the town. It didn't ring true then and it surely doesn't seem likely now.'

Chilcot was on the point of explaining one or two things as touched upon this reputation, when the door to the street opened and three men entered the store.

It was the first time that morning that the store had been completely empty and the three newcomers had an air about them of needing plenty of room. They seemed to fill the place in a way that a dozen ordinary customers did not. As soon as he caught sight of the men, Chilcot knew at once that these were the ones who had been plaguing Jake Pearson's mother and he felt, as a consequence, very ill disposed towards them from the start. It wasn't hard to work out that one was in charge of the other two, because the hulking great fellow with the meanest look about him that Chilcot had seen in a good, long while advanced to the counter, while the other two stood guard at the door. One of these men flicked the latch on the door and turned the sign round to show that the store was now closed for business.

'Mrs Pearson, good day to you. You can guess why we're here.'

Chilcot, who had been tidying up some trays of seeds, stopped what he was doing and came to stand to one side of the counter. He stared hard at the man who had just spoken, so hard in fact that the fellow turned to his right and said, 'What are you lookin' at, old-timer? You the new help or something? If so, make sure to keep out o' things as don't concern you.'

The old man made no reply, but simply watched the younger man intently. Because he was concealed from the waist down by the wooden counter, the man speaking to Mrs Pearson had not marked that the white-haired old man was heeled. He said to the woman, 'We been as patient as Job over this, but time's run out. You causin' us a lot o' grief and either we settle matters here this day or things are like to get ugly.'

'You know what I told you,' said Mrs Pearson. 'You'll not get a cent out of me on a threat. You ought to be ashamed of yourselves, the whole set of you.'

'Yes well, a man's got to earn a livin' somehow.'

This was too much for Chilcot to

bear and he walked round the counter and went up a little closer to the man who was speaking and said quietly, 'A man? You and your friends call yourselves men, do you? That makes strange listenin' when I see you all trying to bully an unprotected woman. Things has changed since I was a young man.'

'When you was a young man Methuselah, we was all living up in the trees!' declared the man, eliciting guffaws of laughter from his friends by the door. 'Now you just stay quiet while I do business with your boss.'

'Business?' asked Chilcot, still in that same, quiet, conversational tone of voice. 'You rascals represent this as a 'business'? Terrorizing folk as work for their living and taking their money from them? I don't think so, not for a moment.'

Up until this moment, the man who was putting the bite on the Widow Pearson had not even turned to face the old fellow who had been working behind the counter and who he took to be some hired help. Now he turned round and looked full at the man and realized for the first time that this softly-spoken old fellow was carrying iron. Not that it signified; there were three of them and only one of him. In addition to which, he looked positively ancient and decrepit into the bargain. 'Don't you get me all riled up, old man. You wouldn't like me when I'm angered.'

'Would I not?' replied Chilcot. 'Well, happen you're right. Mind, that cuts both ways. I don't think you'd care overmuch to see me lose my temper either.' He turned to Mrs Pearson and said, 'I'm guessing here that these are the boys who have been pestering you?' She nodded.

Up to this point, everything had moved along at a relaxed and easygoing pace and anybody looking through the window of the store and not able to hear what was being said, would not have known that anything was amiss; let alone that a woman was being threatened. Then, events jerked forward at breakneck speed, leaving even those three men, who were used to lively action of every description, breathless with surprise.

No sooner had Brook Chilcot received confirmation from Jake's mother that these were the men who had been leaning on her, than he swung into action. Of all types and varieties of men, none was more loathsome in Chilcot's eyes than those who preyed on women. Before the man in front of him had the least idea of his peril, Chilcot had drawn the old-fashioned Navy Colt which he was carrying at his hip, cocked it with his thumb as he was bringing it up and then rammed the barrel hard into the soft part of the bully's throat, just beneath the angle of his jaw. Having done this, he said in a deadly voice, 'What say I blow your brains out, you son of a bitch?'

The reversal of fortunes was so

unexpected and swift that none of the three men knew quite how to deal with this new situation. They were all of them accustomed to menacing others and seeing them shrink back in fear. To find the tables turned like this was a new, alarming and unwelcome experience. Chilcot took the man's arm gently and, still pressing the pistol very hard into his throat, said, 'Even if one o' your friends over yonder should take it into his head to shoot me now, you may be sure I'll still pull the trigger. By the by, I filed down this'un; it's what they call a hair trigger. Tell you the truth, should I so much as cough now, I'm apt to kill you by accident.'

'Don't neither o' you two do anything now,' said the man to his two associates. 'Just let him have his way.'

'That's right good advice,' said Chilcot approvingly. 'I couldn't o' put it better myself. Now you boys just open up that door and step outside, why don't you? Your boss'll follow you out.'

The two of them looked inquiringly

142

at the man who Chilcot was holding hostage, who said in a strangled voice, 'Do as he says.'

The men by the door opened it and left the store. Chilcot said, 'Right, let's you and me take a little stroll now.' He led the man to the doorway, all the while forcing his pistol as hard as he could under the man's jaw. It was painful, but that was not Chilcot's primary purpose; which was to make sure that the barrel was anchored in place and his victim would not be able to jerk his head free. When they reached the door, Chilcot said, 'Now I'm about to let you leave with your life, which is a sight more than you deserve. I'll be covering the three of you and if you think that any of you can draw and fire at me before I'm able to squeeze this trigger, well all I can say is, you go right ahead and try your luck. Walk clear to the end of the street before any of you turn or I'm liable to open fire. Understood? Now get out of here.'

Once he'd joined his two partners,

who were waiting uncertainly in the street outside, he said something in a low voice and all three of them started walking towards Main Street, not one of them so much as glancing at Chilcot. For his part, he kept his pistol out and aimed at their backs, just on the off chance that they didn't have the sense God gave a goat and were minded to turn and draw.

When he went back into the store, it was to find Mrs Pearson as white as a sheet of paper and leaning on the counter, as though she could not support her own weight any more. Chilcot hurried round to the other side of the counter, found the chair and then gently guided her into it. He said, 'My, you just set there for a space, 'til you feel better. Here, I'll fetch you a glass of water.'

When she had sat there for a minute, Jake's mother said, 'I thought there would have been bloodshed.'

'What, with cowards like that? No, trying to push a woman about is one thing, but you won't catch that breed risking their lives if they can help it. They knew I had the drop on 'em.'

'Well, I'm in your debt, Mr Chilcot, but you can't come to work every day with me. They'll be back.'

'Yes,' said Chilcot, rubbing his chin thoughtfully. 'I'd about say that you're right there, ma'am. I should think that they will be back. Let's see what happens, though. There's no point in going to meet trouble halfway, as my old grandpappy used to say.' He looked round the store and said, 'I hope I'm not getting above myself, but I'd say that after that little shock, you need to get home and rest. If you'd let me, I would be happy to tend the store for you this afternoon.'

'You'd do that?'

Chilcot chuckled and said, 'Lordy, ma'am, that ain't nothing. I reckon I could sell brooms and such-like without any bother. Everything's priced up. Why not leave me the keys and you cut along home now?'

'I almost feel that I will. But I can't let you do so much for me like this . . . '

'That's nothing,' Chilcot said gruffly. 'Just hand me your keys and I'll bring 'em back at the end of the day.'

So it was that those living in Grafton's Peak who had not had a chance in the morning to investigate the rumours about the return of Sheriff Chilcot, turned up at the hardware store after noon and discovered that the man himself was serving behind the counter. Brook Chilcot had the air of a man who would not be best pleased if those entering the place for a glimpse of him were to leave with only some token purchase and so the afternoon's customers went off with more substantial items than those who had come to gossip in the morning.

* * *

By about four, the novelty of being treated like some animated waxwork, to be stared at and discussed outside the store, had long worn off for Chilcot and so the old man closed up shop and took the day's takings over to Mrs Pearson's house. When she saw how much money had been taken, Jake's mother was surprised and pleased. 'Well,' she said, 'that certainly makes up for the poor showing this morning. We're about to eat, Mr Chilcot. You'll join us, of course?'

'Thank you, ma'am. I won't deny as I'm a little hungry.'

As soon as the three of them were seated around the table and grace recited, Jake Pearson said, 'What I still can't seem to make out, sir, is why you lost your job after shooting those men. Seems to me like the town would o' been grateful, never mind getting rid of you.'

'Jacob Pearson,' said his mother in a scandalized voice, 'whatever ails you? You just hush your mouth now. Mr Chilcot'll think you had no raising at all, asking such a question.'

As for Chilcot himself, he threw

back his head and laughed out loud. 'Ah, let the boy alone, if you please, ma'am. It's a fair question.' He turned to Jake and said, 'You recollect that I told you how a lot of the less honest types abandoned this town after the death of the Adams brothers, on account of they thought that vigilante law had come to Grafton's Peak?'

'Yes sir, I recall your saying so.'

'That meant a loss for some folk living here. That was irksome to some. Well, then again, I never would have any deputies. Men on the town council would always be recommending this nephew or that, or maybe a son as a likely fellow to assist me and I wouldn't have a one of them. Then, next thing they know, I got my own brother working alongside me as a deputy. Looked to some folks like I was somewhat of a hypocrite.'

'I kind of see all that,' said Jake. 'Was that all?'

'Well, if you discount me starting a gunfight and killing four men who seemingly meant me no harm.'

At that, Mrs Pearson interrupted, saying, 'Meant you no harm? What nonsense is this? Why, one of those men was set on killing you that day!'

'So I thought at the time, ma'am. I was wrong, though.'

'You weren't wrong. I ought to know. My own husband, Jacob here's father, heard it all. If you and your brother hadn't acted as you did, you would have died that day.'

'You got the drop on me here, Mrs Pearson. Could you tell me what you know about that day? I've been sure these twenty years or more that I shot down men needlessly, through a simple misunderstanding.'

8

Mrs Pearson thought for a moment, gathering her ideas together before speaking. Then she said, 'Mind, you have to remember that I was little more than a child myself at the time, I was thirteen and Jacob's father was a year older. Even at that time, we were sweethearts. Dave was working odd afternoons at the Golden Eagle and that's how he heard all this. He was sweeping the floor, putting out the garbage and suchlike. There was an Irisher used to drink there. Mean-looking fellow and I can't for the life of me bring his name to mind. Cagney? Callahan? Something of the sort.'

'Not Cahill, I suppose?' asked Chilcot.

'That's it! Joseph Cahill. He used to be pretty close to Moses Adams from what I heard from David. The day before that big shootout, Dave was tipping some ashes out back of the Golden Eagle and when he went out, he could hear voices. He wasn't precisely eavesdropping, if you take my meaning, but he recognized Moses Adams's voice. Adams and the other fellow were behind a fence, standing in the alley next to the saloon, if you know the layout of the place?'

'I know it well enough,' said Chilcot, listening intently. 'Please go on.'

'Well, Moses said, 'You sure he's going to be there?' and then Dave heard an Irish-sounding voice answer, 'Yes, don't you worry. I'll set him on the trail and he'll be there all right.' Then Moses Adams said, 'Nobody durst lay hands on me. I'll kill him, you'll see. He's going to be too busy watching the others step off that train. He won't know what hit him.' That was all.'

'You mean that your late husband thought that Moses was going to come a-creepin' up behind me while I was expecting trouble from Ike, Jethro and Ezra?'

'Oh yes, that's exactly what he thought. He was going to tell somebody, but like everybody else, he was mortal scared of the Adams brothers. He was only fourteen. He was at the depot that day, you know. Saw the whole thing.'

'Lord, ma'am, I don't lay any blame at the door of your dead husband, may he rest in peace. No, I was just thinking that I've been misled for a good long while. To tell you the truth, I thought that that brother of mine had buffaloed me into committing murder that day. You done lifted a great weight from my shoulders.'

Jake couldn't restrain himself at this point and burst in, saying to his mother, 'But why didn't you tell anybody later? It might o' stopped 'em from taking his job from him.'

'The answer to that,' replied Mrs Pearson, 'is that not a soul knew that there was any question of Mr Chilcot here losing his position. The first we heard was that he had left town and the details only came out later. Sure I told some people, but most preferred to think the worst of a man who was no longer there to defend his reputation.' She turned to Chilcot and said, 'I can only beg your pardon, Mr Chilcot, for not doing more before now to set the record straight.'

But Brook Chilcot hardly heard what she was saying; so enchanted was he to discover that he had not after all needlessly killed those four men. He had in his life shot a fair few men and their deaths had never troubled the old man. Either it had been during the War Between the States or they had been outlaws and criminals. He had never given any of them a second thought. But the notion that he had orphaned a little boy needlessly had been preying on his mind for better than two decades and it surely was a relief to find that those boys had deserved it all along.

Knowing that Moses had been coming up behind him on that fateful afternoon with the intention of killing him put a different complexion upon all the other events that day. No doubt the three other brothers had some idea of what was in the wind. Had they exchanged ciphered telegrams or something of that sort? Whatever it was that had been going on, Chilcot realized that his brother had saved his life and wished that he'd shown some gratitude for it. It was too late now.

'Well, ma'am, I'd say that I'm in your debt for this. You've set my mind at ease over a matter which has unsettled me these many years. I owe you a favour.'

'Why, don't be absurd,' said Mrs Pearson. 'Maybe I should have spoke out louder and earlier. I'm sure you have no occasion to feel in my debt.'

'Well, but I do. The least I can do before leaving town is to settle up this little problem of yours and send those rats scuttling back to their burrows.'

On hearing this proposal, Jake's mother looked seriously alarmed. She said urgently, 'Really, I beg that you will do nothing of the sort. There's more to the case than meets the eye. It's not just a band of villains. The sheriff himself is mixed up with this in some way.'

'Ah,' said Chilcot, 'so it's a case of the apple not falling far from the tree, is that how it is? Tell me about Ike Adams's boy. He can't be more than thirty, thirty-two by my reckoning. That's young for a sheriff.'

'Jacob, take these dishes out to the kitchen and wash them, please,' said his mother abruptly. 'Me and Mr Chilcot are going to take a turn around the garden. I'm sure he would like to see my herbs.'

Catching her drift at once, Chilcot said, 'Why yes, ma'am, that's right. I'm a rare one for gardening.'

Once they were out of the house, Mrs Pearson said firmly, 'It's very kind of you and I truly do appreciate your aid today, but I can't let you get mixed up in affairs here. I must tackle them myself.'

Had she known him a little longer, the woman might have been suspicious of the mild way in which Chilcot agreed at once with her, begging her only to tell him a little about how things were situated in Grafton's Peak these days, just for old times' sake. There was a seat at one end of the tiny garden and they sat upon this. The evening air was fragrant with the scent of flowers and herbs, the cultivation and care of which were Mrs Pearson's especial joy and pleasure.

'Really, things aren't too bad these days in the town. Better than they used to be. Keith Tranter's a sly piece of work, but he keeps the town quiet. I've my own views on him, but that's another matter.'

'What about those fellows this morning?' asked Chilcot. 'They anything to do with him?'

'It may be so. The amounts of money they're taking aren't ruinously great and other businesses are treating it almost like an additional tax. It's true that since Tranter became sheriff, things are more peaceful than ever on the streets. If paying a little more in a sort of tax than usual is the price of it, then I'd say most folks might accept it.'

'But not you, ma'am?'

'I'm a woman. It's not to be expected that I should be so willing to turn a blind eye to the one racket that is still going on round here, just because it doesn't affect folk in the town. Maybe everything else is taking place away from town, but this is right under our eyes and we tolerate it.'

'I'm sorry Mrs Pearson, but you've lost me now. You mean this collecting money from store owners and so on?'

'No, I'm talking about something quite different. I mean the trafficking of young girls which carries on through this very town. What they call 'white slaving'.'

'You'll think me slow, but that doesn't mean a whole lot to me.'

'Men go round farms and sign up girls, country girls, ignorant things who don't understand the world. They tell them that they're going to be singers or actresses and such, then take them to somewhere out of reach of the law. The lucky ones end up as saloon girls; others are forced to become, well, to work in houses of ill repute.'

'I've heard of this,' said Chilcot grimly, 'but not as 'white slaving'. It's the devil's work. You say this town is a staging route for such unfortunate young women? Where do they fetch up, Mexico?'

'Yes, Mexico.'

'Nobody in the town object to this, other than you?'

'The girls aren't being coerced. They're all happy enough to go south, poor fools. People here don't see it as their business when they see parties of these young women passing through. 'Sides which, it's good business for people here. There's clothes bought for the girls, liquor and tobacco too, which is smuggled over the border at the same time as the girls. You know the Mexicans have a harsh system of taxation and duty on things. Cross the

Rio Grande and you can sell a bottle of whiskey or pound of tobacco for almost twice what you paid for it here and the fellow buying it in Mexico is still getting it cheaper than he would in a store there. Those accompanying those silly young girls always stock up on spirits when they pass through town.'

'Well, ma'am, you've opened my eyes. If you'll allow me to trespass on your hospitality for a day or two longer, then I think I'll look into this and see if I can't persuade those mixed up in it to reconsider their actions. I don't much object to smuggling liquor. I won't say as I haven't benefited from such trade myself in the past, but there's nothing worse than transporting women around for immoral purposes and if it's being tolerated here, then it shouldn't be and that's all I'll say on the subject.'

'Mr Chilcot, you are very welcome to stay here as long as you wish. For bringing my son back safely, I owe you a great deal. But please don't feel that you have to involve yourself in anything, not on my account.'

★   ★   ★

It felt very strange to be walking into the Golden Eagle for the first time in twenty-two years. The décor didn't look to Chilcot to have changed all that much since last he had been there. Then again, what would be the point of spending a heap of money on such an enterprise as doing up the saloon differently? This was how those who drank at the Golden Eagle had always liked the place to be and that was probably still the case. Why change a winning bet?

'What can I get you?' asked the barkeep.

The temptation to ask for a whiskey was suddenly all but overwhelming. What would be the harm in just one drink? 'Get thee behind me, Satan!' muttered Chilcot.

'I'm sorry, friend, I didn't quite catch

that?' said the barkeep, looking at him oddly.

'No matter. Do you have such a thing as a pitcher of buttermilk?' The fellow behind the bar stared at Chilcot as though he had never heard anything so strange in all his life. 'Come, you know what buttermilk is, I'll warrant. Do you have some?' said Chilcot irritably.

'I'll go check.'

As it happened, there was buttermilk in the kitchen, although judging from the look on the man's face, this was probably the first time he had ever been asked for such a drink.

Once he had had his glass of milk, Chilcot turned to survey the barroom. The saloon was fairly busy, but not crowded. There were several groups of men clustered at tables and he had the impression that these men were engaged in business, rather than having come there to relax over a few drinks. One group in particular caught his eye, consisting of three white men and the same number of swarthy and dark-skinned types, who Chilcot took to be Mexicans. He studied the men at the table for a while, wondering if they were some of those who were engaged in this racket of which Mrs Pearson had spoken.

The old man's motives that evening were fairly straightforward. On the one hand, he had a genuine and abiding hatred of those who mistreated women. The news that there was some crooked business involving forced prostitution, which operated in some way out of Grafton's Peak, truly horrified him. Then again, he felt that he could hardly leave town now, knowing that as soon as he left, those men he had crossed swords with that morning would be back to terrorize young Jake's mother. No, it wasn't to be thought of. For both these reasons, he had decided that he would clear up one or two things before going home.

Brook Chilcot had a third motive; one composed entirely of self-interest. Until a few days ago, he had been a sad and largely useless old man with a weakness for liquor, who had of late been reduced to begging drinks from strangers. Now, he had a purpose and a job of work to do; the first in several years. He had brought that foolish boy back home, prevented the passengers on the Katy Flyer from being robbed and seen off the men who were threatening Mrs Pearson. As a consequence, Chilcot felt better about himself than he had for years. He was useful again. Once he hopped on that train back to Endurance, he would fade back into obscurity and, most likely, dipsomania. It wasn't to be borne! He would stay right here as long as he could be some good to others and at the same time be worth something to himself.

One thing that Chilcot had observed time and again in his days as a lawman was that one sort of villainy often went hand in hand with another. The man who today was robbing a stage would tomorrow be cooking up moonshine or running a string of whores. He would take oath that the men he'd driven out of the store today probably had a finger in this detestable trade in women as well. They certainly looked the type. Besides which, if the sheriff here was allowing some kind of regulated extortion of honest businessmen, then he must surely be taking a rake-off from other criminal activity in the town.

Chilcot shook his head sadly. He thought that the days of the badman sheriff were over. It was surprising to find such a man these days. And yet, considering the antecedents of this particular sheriff, it was not wholly unlooked for. As soon as he had learned whose son the sheriff of Grafton's Peak was, he might at once have expected to discover that the man was up to no good.

These melancholy reflections were brought to an abrupt end when the batwing doors leading to the street outside were pulled open and through them stepped the very man who

Chilcot had offered to kill earlier that day. The fellow spotted Chilcot at once and came ambling over in his direction; the expression on his face indicating that he wished to bandy a few words with the former sheriff of Grafton's Peak.

Oddly enough, Chilcot was by no means displeased to see the man heading towards him. Quite the contrary, in fact. His recent train of thought had led him towards the idea that those who had come into the hardware store that day were like as not involved in any other bad things going on hereabouts. The man who was bearing down on him right now, probably with the intention of murdering him, could be the very one to help him out.

'Hallo there,' Chilcot greeted the man affably. 'Can I buy you a drink?'

'I got a crow to pluck with you, fellow,' said the man. 'Never mind about anybody buying drinks, nor nothing of the sort.'

This didn't sound too promising, but Chilcot was a man who, once he was set upon a course, did not readily deviate from it. He said, 'I can see as you're a mite upset after that little episode this morning. Can't say as I blame you, neither. Still, this is business I want to talk with you. All's said and done, we wasn't neither of us hurt today, which is a mercy.'

The man seemed anything but appeased by these words, remarking, 'I'm strongly minded to rip your head from your body.'

'You could do that, but then you might miss out on a heap o' money.'

At the magic word 'money', the man's urge to destroy Chilcot on the spot contended with his cupidity and greed and he stood vacillating for a moment, unable to figure out which was the stronger motive for action. All this was hugely satisfying for Chilcot, because it confirmed his opinion about the man standing irresolutely before him. As he had suspected, the fellow was both unintelligent and indecisive; just exactly as Chilcot had hoped.

'Tell you what,' said Chilcot, 'why don't I buy you a drink and let you know what's what. Then if it don't accord to our mutual satisfaction, why then you can rip off my head anyways?' He stuck out his hand and said, 'Brook W. Chilcot at your service, sir.'

With evident reluctance, the other grasped his hand and mumbled, 'Catesby.' Chilcot never learned whether that was his Christian or surname and the owner of the name did not feel called upon to enlighten him.

'A large glass of whiskey for my friend here!' Chilcot called to the barkeep. Catesby had in the meantime been staring at the creamy white liquid in Chilcot's own glass. He asked, 'What in the hell you got there?'

'That? It's milk. You know, stuff as comes out o' cows.'

When the whiskey arrived, Chilcot paid for it and then suggested that the two of them should go over to a quiet corner and talk business. To which Catesby replied, 'I ain't yet made up my mind not to kill you for what you done this day.'

'Well, there'll be time enough for that later. I'm goin' nowhere.'

Once they were seated together at a table, some distance from the other patrons of the Golden Eagle, Catesby said, 'Well? What's this all about?'

'I've a suspicion that as well as putting the bite on storekeepers, you trade in young women. Girls and such, that you help ferry down south to cathouses across the border. Am I right?'

Even before Catesby opened his mouth, Chilcot could see that his guess had been right on the money. The burly and slow-witted individual was looking hard at him and made no attempt to deny the suggestion. He said, 'What if I am? What's it to you?'

'Ah, sharp man. Straight to the point. I like that. Here it is, then. I've got a considerable sum o' money as

I've gathered over the years. Now I want to put it to work. I know the profits on that game of transportin' women across to Mexico. I want to invest in it. Be like what they call a 'sleeping partner'.'

Catesby had the kind of face which showed at once what was going on in the owner's mind. It would, thought Chilcot, have been pure pleasure to have a few hands of poker with such a man; you couldn't lose! In the present case, the desire to hurt Chilcot, which had dominated Catesby's expression up 'til now, briefly gave way to a look of greed when money was mentioned. Then, the two expressions combined into one and the stupid, ox-like individual sitting in front of Chilcot almost smiled. It was very plain what he was thinking now; that he could somehow steal the money of which Chilcot was talking and then kill the owner of the money anyway.

Chilcot thought to himself that he hadn't lost any of the skills which had stood him in such good stead as a lawman. He had read this fellow perfectly and now hooked him without any trouble at all.

Catesby said, 'How much money might we be a talkin' of here?'

'A shade over eight thousand dollars. That buy me a piece of this action that you got going on down here?'

'I should think it just about might,' said Catesby, almost unable to smother a grin. 'Yes, I think we might let you into the game for a stake like that. Mind, you'll need to talk to my boss about it first.'

'Your boss?' Chilcot feigned amazement. 'Why, I quite apprehended that you were the head of this outfit. You mean there's somebody above you?'

'Not above,' said Catesby, his pride affronted by the notion. 'No, he ain't above me. But he holds the reins of one or two things, on account of his special position.'

'Special position? I don't rightly understand you.'

'You will do, when you meet him. Where's this money o' yourn? You got it with you now?'

'What, eight thousand dollars? You think I'd carry it round in my saddle-bag? No, I can wire to Kansas and get it transferred down here as soon as you like, if we come to an agreement.'

Catesby finished his drink and stood up. 'There's no time like now. You want to come with me?'

The two men left the saloon and Catesby led the former sheriff down a side street which ran towards the depot. They arrived at a battered, nondescript door in an alleyway, upon which Catesby rapped imperiously. It was opened by one of the men who had accompanied him to Mrs Pearson's store. This fellow looked astounded to see Chilcot, evidently recognizing him at once. Catesby said, 'Is the boss here?'

'Yeah, he's in the other room. What's . . . ?'

'I'll tell you all later,' promised

Catesby. He turned to Chilcot and said, 'Come on. This way.'

The room into which Chilcot was led was small and cramped. It had only one small window, which was set high up in the wall and protected by bars. He hardly noticed this though, because his attention was focused upon the man sitting behind a table; upon which were piled various books and ledgers. When he entered the room, this man looked up and a smile spread across his face, although without ever quite reaching his eyes. 'Hallo, Sheriff Chilcot,' he said. 'It's been a good long while.'

Chilcot found himself gazing into the cold blue eyes of Ike Adams's son.

9

Chilcot was not altogether overcome with shock to learn that Keith Tranter was working hand in glove with, or even directing, criminal activity in Grafton's Peak. In truth, it was no more than he had expected. Tranter said, 'I reckon that one of my boys will take charge of that pistol of yours, Mr Chilcot. I get a mite nervous when folk that massacred my kith and kin are standing in front of me with a gun near at hand. Catesby, just pull that antique from his holster, would you? If he offers resistance, kill him.'

'This is a fine way to treat a man who's just offered to put a heap of money into your enterprise,' said Chilcot angrily. 'I thought better of you than to hold a grudge so long. I'd heard you were a man of business first and foremost.'

'What's all this?' Tranter asked of the man who had led Chilcot to him. Catesby outlined briefly what had been suggested to him; about the eight thousand dollars that Chilcot was offering to invest. When he had set this out to his boss, Tranter declared roundly, 'That sounds like a lot of crap to me. That old man looks to me as though he'd have trouble paying his rent, never mind having thousands of dollars squirreled away somewhere. We'll see.'

Chilcot felt that it was time that he took control of the situation. He said, 'I come here in good faith to join in your business. You don't want my money, I'll just leave right now.' He turned to go.

Keith Tranter said, 'Bind him hand and foot. If he offers any trouble, knock him senseless. Don't kill him, though. I want to do that myself later.' There was something extraordinarily chilling about the casual, conversational tone in which the sheriff of Grafton's Peak spoke. It put Chilcot strongly in mind of the young man's father, who had spoken in a similarly detached and unemotional fashion about violence and killing. Chilcot whirled angrily to Tranter and began to protest. He saw the man nod to somebody behind Chilcot and then he was struck hard on the back of his head and the blackness rose up and engulfed him.

When he came round, it was to find that his hands were securely bound behind his back and his ankles also lashed together. Chilcot was still in the same room where he had spoken to Tranter, but now it was deserted. There was little point in shouting; for all he knew to the contrary, the nearest men would turn out to be cronies of Tranter. The most noise he could make was a muted grunting. There was not the least possibility of making himself heard by anybody outside the room. Well, Brook, he thought to himself, you surely are in a pickle this time. You would have done better to think things through a little before acting, which has been your downfall in the past.

At a guess, Tranter and his men would by now be trying to find out where Chilcot was staying in town. If there was any real prospect of getting their hands on a substantial sum of money, then they would probably even now be dreaming up a scheme, by which they would both possess themselves of this fictional eight thousand dollars and then do away with him at roughly the same time. Once they found, as they surely must before long, that it was all nonsense about his having a heap of money, then Keith Tranter would most likely just kill him and get his friends to dispose of the corpse somewhere. Both possibilities seemed to end with Chilcot's death, which was a sobering and disheartening thought.

There was only one chance, although an incredibly slender one. When he was a much younger man, Brook Chilcot had been accustomed to carry a small muff pistol concealed about his person. He always carried this hidden weapon in addition to whatever he might have been sporting in the usual way of things, such as rifles and revolvers. It was a habit which he had maintained throughout his years working in law enforcement and only dropped when he had more or less retired for good some years before.

Before boarding the train to bring young Jake Pearson home, it had pleased Chilcot's vanity to strap on his old pistol and also to clip the derringer inside his boot. He had laughed to himself as he did so, but now Chilcot wondered if he'd had a premonition or something. The big question was whether or not he would even be able to reach the damned thing, never mind fire it.

There was a throbbing pain in his skull and Chilcot could feel that the sparse hair on the crown of his head was sticky with congealing blood, which had oozed over his head and run down his cheek while he was unconscious. All he really felt like doing was lying back and resting. Even had he wished to do so, this would have been impossible. His wrists were so tightly bound that Chilcot began to worry that the circulation might be cut off if he didn't free them soon. There was nothing for it but to wriggle about like an eel and see if he couldn't get his hands down to his boot and pull out that titchy little pistol.

Some years ago, Chilcot had visited a carnival sideshow which featured a man called the human snake. This fellow had been born without arms and the range of things he could do with his feet and mouth was purely amazing. He'd needed to wriggle about a fair bit, but this singular individual had been able to get dressed by his self and even shave, holding the razor with his toes. As he contorted his body now, throwing himself from side to side, Chilcot thought that he must look a little like that human snake himself.

At last, with one last convulsive jerk, Chilcot succeeded in driving his bound hands backwards and extracting the derringer from where it nestled in the top of his boot. What a mercy those bastards didn't think to search me, he thought. Figured maybe as I was too old to cause 'em any trouble, did they? Well, let's see. Having got the pistol gripped in his hands, which were still twisted cruelly behind his back, Chilcot's next difficulty was to find a way of shooting anybody with it. It was a double-barrelled, over-and-under piece, but he'd most likely only have a chance for one shot.

After some experimenting, which left the old man shaking and breathless with the exertion, Chilcot managed to work out a way. He manoeuvred himself until he was lying on his back, with his head touching the wall which faced the only door into the room. He found that if he kicked his legs up as high as they would go from this position, he had a brief moment when the pistol had an unobstructed field of fire, under his buttocks and in the direction of the door. Mind, he thought wryly, I'd best time this right, else I'm going to end by shooting my balls off!

Lying on his back in this way was about as uncomfortable a position as it was possible to maintain, but it was important to be ready and waiting. Of course, if a whole bunch of men came to get him, then he was dead anyway. His only hope was that just one man would enter the room in which he was being held captive.

There was no way to gauge the passing of time, but from the fact that it was probably nearly dark outside that little window, Chilcot calculated that it was perhaps half eight or thereabouts. As he considered this point, he thought that he heard a soft click in the next room; the one which he had entered through the door in that alleyway. He kept perfectly still, straining every nerve to see if he had imagined that furtive noise. Then there came the sound of footsteps and in another moment the door opened and into the room came the man he knew as Catesby. He was alone, which was more than Chilcot could have hoped for.

'Boss says as we ain't to kill you,' said Catesby, 'but I can't see that it would do any harm to hurt you some. Be a pleasure to do so. You made a fool out o' me this morning.'

'You don't need my help as far as that goes,' Chilcot told him, 'I'd say you manage to make a fool of yourself just fine without anybody doing a thing.'

'You just shut your mouth, mister. I'm goin' to show you what happens to men like you, men as don't know how to behave theyselves.'

'You'll need help. I can't see you whipping me by yourself. Best call your friends in to aid you.'

'There ain't nobody but you and me, buster. I can deal with a whore's son like you by my own self.'

'Thanks,' said Chilcot. 'That's all I needed to know.' He kicked his legs as high as they would go, leaving the muff pistol grasped behind his back a clear field to the bully standing but six feet away. When his legs were at their highest point, Chilcot fired. He did not, as he had feared he might, end up mutilating his private parts with the .44 bullet. Instead, it flew straight and true into Catesby's breast.

The roar of the gun was deafening in the enclosed space. Through the whisps of blue smoke, Chilcot could see that the big man was still standing there, looking down at him balefully. For a dreadful moment, he thought that he had missed, but then Catesby said, 'You done killed me!'

'I surely hope so,' replied Chilcot and had the immense satisfaction of seeing the man in front of him sway to and fro, before crashing to the floor. 'I thought you'd never die,' said Chilcot, more to himself than to Catesby. 'Now let's hope and pray that you have a knife about you, otherwise I'm not much better off than I was before.'

It was an enormous relief to find the jack-knife which Catesby had been carrying. Opening it and sawing through his bonds was no easy task and as the blood began to flow again through his wrists, the spasm of pain took Chilcot's breath away. He muttered an obscene oath and then hacked away at the rawhide thong which secured his ankles together. Once that was done he stood up and then had to sit down again swiftly. He felt giddy and sick.

There was no time to lose and even if it meant crawling out of there on his hands and knees, then he knew that he had to get moving at once. The dead man was sporting a fancy .45, with ivory grips. It was a double-action piece, which didn't suit Chilcot's inclinations, but this was most definitely one of those times when beggars can't be choosers. He tucked the pistol in his own empty holster, but it didn't fit too well. His old .36 Navy was a deal slimmer and the holster he had on was tailored to fit a Colt Navy. Well, it couldn't be helped.

Having freed himself and appropriated Catesby's weapon, it only remained to make tracks out of there as soon as could be. There was nobody around and Chilcot slipped up the narrow space between the buildings and soon found himself on Main Street. He didn't think it wise to head towards the Golden Eagle and so worked his way round behind the stores until he came near to the Pearsons' house. This was as far as he'd been able to plan. Since leaving there a few short hours ago, he had confirmed everything which had before been only vague suspicions and his lawman's instincts. He knew now that the sheriff of Grafton's Peak was in charge of at least two of the rackets and also that Ike Adams's son would be coming to kill him at the first opportunity. At the least, he needed to warn Jake's mother about what had chanced since last he saw her.

A gentle rap on the glass panes of the

front door brought forth Mrs Pearson. She took one look at the old man and her hand flew to her mouth in shock. 'Lord, whatever's 'come of you, Mr Chilcot? You're all over blood.'

'If I could impose upon you for just a short time, ma'am,' said Chilcot, 'I hope soon to be out of your hair altogether and for good.'

Recovering her poise, Jake's mother said briskly, 'You best come straight into the kitchen and let me clean up your head. You've certainly been in the wars.'

'It's not as bad as it looks. You know how a little blood makes much of itself.'

Once they were in the kitchen, Chilcot sat down and allowed the woman to fuss around him with a basin of warm water, sponging away the sticky, half-dried blood from his matted scalp. 'Somebody strike you from behind?'

'That's just so, ma'am. A regular coward's trick. I've every confidence, though, that the person as did it won't be serving another after the same fashion.'

Mrs Pearson stopped cleaning Chilcot's hair and stared into his face. 'You can't mean that . . . ?'

'I won't deceive you,' said Chilcot slowly, 'not with you giving me hospitality in your home like this. There's been a killing and if I'm any judge o' such things, there'll be more this night.'

The woman continued mopping the dried blood away and said, 'Please tell me, Mr Chilcot, that this bloodshed isn't all on my account? You're not doing all this for me?'

To her surprise, the old man laughed out loud at that; a long, rich chuckle of genuine amusement. He said, 'Well, I won't say as I wasn't glad to settle with that bully that troubled you this morning. I'd be a liar if I said else wise. But no, it's not really for you. It's for me, for my own self.'

'How so?'

'It's like this, Mrs Pearson. When I

was sheriff here, I turned a blind eye to much that I shouldn't have. There was gun-running down into Mexico and up into the Indian Nations, moonshining, liquor smuggling, illegal bullion movement and I don't know what all else. Grafton's Peak prospered on such things and as long as the streets were decent and safe for the women of the town to walk down, well then we let the badmen get along with it.'

The woman tending to Chilcot's scalp gave a brief laugh and said, 'Sounds just like today. I'm telling you, those farm girls being taken south, they all get kitted out here with new clothes and bonnets and suchlike. Half the trade in dry goods goes in that direction.'

'Well then you'll most likely take my point, ma'am. I went along with all that then, when I should have been coming down hard, whether or no the things were taking place right under my nose here in Grafton's Peak. Soon as I put down my foot and scared off all those rascals and sent them to another town, people here lost a heap of business and they didn't forgive me for it.'

'It's the self-same thing today. There's twenty girls arrived this day. They're putting up at the old commercial hotel. You know the place?'

'Yes, just across from the depot, as I recall.'

'Those poor, young fools are as bright and excited as you could wish. All of 'em think they're going to make their fortunes on the stage or some such nonsense. They'll be here in town for a few days, until they've all got new outfits, and then they'll be off south. It's a scandal that we tolerate it.'

Mrs Pearson went to a drawer and came back with a roll of bandage. Chilcot said, 'No, thank you, ma'am. The fresh air's best for cuts and bruises.' He stood up. 'As for this scandal that you talk of, I couldn't agree with you more. But I can tell you now that if I have anything to do with it, you won't have to put up with it after tonight. I mean to do what I should have done twenty years ago and clean up some of the dirt and filth. I can't think of a better place to begin than this vile traffic in young girls.'

There was a braced determination in the old man which shone out. Looking at him now, Jake's mother half believed that this white-haired man might be capable of dealing with the corruption which afflicted the town. She said, 'Jacob is at his friend's house. You will come back here to bid him farewell? Before you leave town, I mean?'

'I'll do my very best, ma'am. My only purpose now is to speak a few words with that precious sheriff of yours and advise him to resign his post and seek new employment; for preference, some good long way from here. I might suggest that he takes some of his friends along with him.'

'You're serious, aren't you?'

'Never was more serious in my life.'

As Chilcot headed for the front door,

Mrs Pearson followed him and said, 'Please take a care of yourself, Mr Chilcot. I surely hope that you don't come to harm.'

★　★　★

The hotel standing near to the railroad station had been built a year or so before Chilcot had been appointed sheriff of Grafton's Peak. The original idea was that it would be a commercial hotel for travelling salesmen, businessmen and so on, but that wasn't how it worked out. There is slow money, the sort that accumulates gradually as a result of honest enterprise, and then again there is fast money; that which piles up rapidly through gambling, crime or shifty and dishonest activities. Somewhere in the history of Grafton's Peak, the inhabitants seemed to have inclined towards the fast money, rather than the slow. It was a good arrangement for the town, as far as it went.

At the time that Chilcot had been

sheriff of Grafton's Peak, the town had been very popular with various kinds of shady character; those who 'toiled not, neither did they spin'. These men would use the town as a base for their activities, always being careful not to outrage the citizens by harming anybody actually living in Grafton's Peak. They spent freely, tipped heavily and brought a lot of money into the place. As long as you didn't inquire too closely into what those fellows were planning to do with the rifles that they bought in town or the liquor which they transported towards the Mexican border or any one of a dozen other dubious transactions, things got along just fine.

The Commercial, as everybody in town called it, had been the regular haunt of those men running the various enterprises being conducted outside the town boundaries. The men who stayed at the Commercial were smart, well-dressed, polite and no trouble to anybody at all in Grafton's Peak. As sheriff, Chilcot had privately viewed the establishment as a pest hole, but as long as nothing occurred on the streets, the town council indicated strongly to him that he should just give the hotel a wide berth and get on with his tax assessments and so on.

It was dark now, but the Commercial was ablaze with light. It looked to Chilcot as though there must be lamps burning in every room of the hotel. As he drew closer to it, he could hear the sound of merry-making. Those girls were surely having a gay old time, believing that the men drinking with them were their best friends and helping them set their feet on the path leading to fame and fortune. If they only knew the truth of the matter! Years ago, Chilcot had been involved in putting a stop to something very similar to this, when a bunch of comancheros were holding up stages, seizing any pretty girls and then taking them down to El Paso, from where they were ferried to brothels deep in Mexico. His hatred of this business at that time had taken a very practical form. He and his posse had hanged every mother's son of those comancheros when once they caught up with them. News of this had reached others minded to engage in the same beastliness and the racket had died out for a spell; at least in that part of Texas where Brook W. Chilcot's writ ran.

Looking now at the Commercial and listening to all the singing and gaiety, it struck Chilcot that he might be on the point of teaching a similar lesson to a new group of those cowardly and unmanly devils. Well, so be it.

10

It was plain that marching straight into the Commercial and challenging the men within to a straight fight would be little better than a dramatic suicide. In there, with the place so brightly illuminated and all of them together, the advantage lay entirely with the men he was going up against. Chilcot knew that he must find a way to lure them out and maybe even up the odds somewhat. Of course, he could shoot up at the windows and draw them out into the darkness, but then he was keenly aware that he had only one pistol and no spare ammunition for it. He couldn't afford to waste a single shot.

The germ of an idea came to him. It was the only one he had, so he hoped devoutly that it might prove a good one. The Golden Eagle had not changed substantially since he had been sheriff here, all those years ago. Maybe the situation was the same for the Commercial? If so, then he might be able to get those men to fight on his own terms and take one of them out at the start, before the fighting got hot.

Although most homes in Grafton's Peak now seemed to have piped drinking water, sanitation did not appear to have altered for the better since his own days here. Most every home relied upon an outside privy. Would the Commercial have gone to the expense of installing something more up to date and modern? Chilcot walked casually round the side of the building and rejoiced to find that five wooden booths still served the bodily needs of the patrons of the Commercial. So far so good.

The next question to tackle was the extent to which all the men in that little hotel were mixed up in the business of those girls. Obviously there were staff there who just tended the bar and cleaned the rooms. It would be ethically wrong and strategically unsound to shoot one of them. All else apart, he could ill afford to expend ammunition needlessly on shooting a bootblack or something of that sort. Nor was Chilcot, at this late stage of his life, inclined to violate the rattlesnake code by killing a man unawares without challenging him first and allowing him a chance to defend himself. He sat down at back of the hotel and reasoned the matter out.

First off was where the staff at the Commercial weren't likely to be carrying. Not that Chilcot would go after an unarmed man anyway, but it simplified matters. What of those who did have guns and came out of that place? Were any of them likely to have nothing to do with the business going on there; that to do with taking those young women south? Chilcot didn't think so. Most probably was that the girls and the men travelling with them had taken over the whole place for a night or two. Still and all, Chilcot figured it just possible that some fellow from town who was nothing at all to do with this filthy trade might just have popped into the Commercial for a glass of porter. It wouldn't be right to challenge such a one. Then it struck him. Those Mexican-looking types he'd seen earlier that day. No doubt some Mexicans would be involved in actually getting those girls to their final destination on the other side of the Rio Grande. Any Mexicans making whoopee with those girls this night would be certain-sure to be connected in some way with what was going on and therefore fair game.

Even now, with so much at stake and the odds so heavily stacked against him, Chilcot would not have dreamed of acting the part of an assassin. He would give the man whose death would be the trigger for the rescue of those little fools a fair chance. He sat in the shadows at the back of the hotel for a good half hour. The first man who came out to the row of privies was bringing a chamber pot to empty. Next were two girls and then another man who wasn't heeled.

At last a swarthy great brute emerged from the rear door of the Commercial. Chilcot saw him silhouetted in the brightly lit doorway for a moment. The fellow looked like the sort of caricature of a Mexican bandit such as you might see on the cover of a dime novel. He even had a bandolier of cartridges slung over one shoulder. This unattractive individual lurched out and disappeared into one of the shabby wooden booths. He looked to Chilcot to be three parts intoxicated, but that was nothing to the purpose. He'd just have to take his chance.

Rodriguez was looking forward to getting home. He generally had a good time with the Yankees, but they weren't his own people. He and his fellow countrymen always had to speak English when they were on a trip like this; the *gringos* got very suspicious if he and his friends spoke Spanish to each other; they always thought that the

Mexicans were hatching some plot against them. For tonight though, Rodriguez was happy. There was one of those girls, a bright, merry little thing, that he intended to have for his self before dawn.

When he had finished making water, Rodriguez stumbled out of the privy to find a man standing no more than ten feet in front of him. 'Hey, man,' Rodriguez said, 'you having good time, no?'

The man considered the question for a second and then said, 'To speak plainly, no. No, I wouldn't say I'm having a good time at all. I never do when I find myself close to a bunch of men who seduce and violate women and children and are next door to being slave traders.'

'What? What do you say?'

'I say you're a stinking bandit, who deserves to die. You want to prove me wrong?'

In his drink-befuddled state, it took Rodriguez a time to work out the play and realize that this old man in front of him was insulting him with the clear aim of provoking him into engaging in a *duello*. The Mexican went for his gun, but was dead before he'd even cleared the holster.

Chilcot didn't waste any time, but went over to the body which had fallen to the ground with a crash. He took the dead man's gun and tucked it into his belt. Then he faded back into the shadows to see what the reaction would be.

The noise of the party was raucous and the drinking heavy, but the sound of a nearby gunshot still caused those inside the hotel to stop their talking for a moment and listen carefully. When there were no more shots, they carried on with the drinking and dancing. A minute later, a youngster who had left to go out back came running in and announced, 'Somebody's shot Rodriguez!'

'Shot him? Is he badly hurt?'

'You might say so. He's stone dead.'

The girls began to give little screams, which were more of pleasurable excitement than genuine fear or alarm. Hearing that a man was shot was just one more novel incident in the adventurous life they'd been leading since being recruited from the dirt farms of Kansas or the Oklahoma Territory. This was just another thrilling part of the trip to fame and fortune in Mexico.

'Shut up, you women,' said one of the men. 'Just shut your mouths and keep silent!' There was dead silence; even the pianist apprehended that something was seriously wrong. The fellow who had told the girls to shut up said to two other men, 'You two, Carter and Brand, you come along of me. Turn down those lamps, the rest of you, and keep away from the windows.'

To the shock of the girls, the fellows who had until a minute or two earlier seemed the most amiable and good-natured of souls now drew their pistols and looked as though they were prepared for any kind of violence. This was an unexpected development. These girls had until fairly recently never been more than five miles from the farms where they had grown up. Some of them had not even possessed before meeting these boys any proper clothes; it being not in the least degree uncommon for girls of fourteen and fifteen to wear adapted flour sacks when at home. In the last couple of weeks, their lives had been transformed and they had lived in a whirl of pleasure; being provided with new dresses and plied with strong liquor and anything else they might require. They were in fact, all unwittingly, being corrupted and prepared for a life of prostitution. Through all this, the men who had persuaded them to come away had behaved as pleasantly as you like; as though they were amiable and good-natured men. Now, they had thrown off that guise and were revealing their true natures.

The three men, guns in their hands,

loped out of the back door of the Commercial, after having taken the precaution of extinguishing all the lamps in the room from which they exited. This meant that their night-sight wasn't hopelessly marred. It would still take ten or fifteen minutes for their ability to see clearly in the dim light to reach the level of that possessed by the old man crouched behind the low stone wall which marked the boundary of the hotel grounds. After all, he had been out in the dark night for nearly an hour.

Chilcot saw the three men with perfect clarity as they came out to investigate the corpse lying nigh to the row of privies. His natural impulse would have been to shout a challenge to the men and call upon them to throw down their weapons, but he knew that this would simply cost him his own life, and that right speedily. His code of honour in these matters was scrupulous, but flexible. They must know by this time that they were under attack and that the onus was upon them to demonstrate to their pursuer that they had surrendered. They gave no indication that this was the way that their minds were tending. Indeed, from all that Chilcot was able to collect, these men were intent upon violence. They peered out into the gloom, their guns in their hands, as though seeking somebody at whom they could direct their fire.

Without making any sudden movements, Chilcot very slowly drew down on the men as they stood over the body of the man he had earlier shot. One of them crouched down and then stood up again, saying in a puzzled voice, 'That's blazing strange. His gun's nowhere to be seen.' These words were the last that Jack Carter ever spoke in the whole course of his life, because at that moment, Chilcot fired. The .45 that he had taken earlier from Catesby was of a considerably greater calibre than his Colt Navy and the recoil was accordingly stronger than he had budgeted for. Instead of hitting his man in the middle of his chest, as Chilcot had aimed to do, the kick of the piece caused the ball to hit about a foot higher, right in the fellow's face. Not that Chilcot saw this, because as soon as he had loosed off the shot, he ducked down and scuttled along the wall.

Because their attention had been focused altogether on the body of their former comrade, neither of the two surviving men standing over Rodriguez's corpse saw the flash of the shot which killed Carter. All they knew was that there was a crack and then the man standing at their side raised a hand uncertainly to his face, looked a bit puzzled and then dropped dead at their feet.

'Shit!' exclaimed Tom Brand. 'We best get under cover.'

The two men threw themselves to the ground and crawled over to the privies. It was an unenviable position in which they found themselves: out in the open on a dark night, being stalked by an unknown number of assailants who appeared to be ready and willing to kill any or all of them.

Chilcot was feeling his age. Running along bent double like that had played hell with his back, which was prone lately to ache at any untoward exertion. He muttered to himself, 'You surely are getting too old for this game, Brook. You ought to be leaving these high jinks to the youngsters.' He peeped cautiously over the top of the wall and found that he could not see either of the other men now; the privies obscured his view. All his hesitations and doubts about the propriety of attacking those men or anybody else in the Commercial had evaporated. They knew by now that they were under attack and so Chilcot felt free to take any shots he could; even at their backs. Abiding by the rattlesnake code was one thing; he wasn't about to play a gunfight according to the Queensbury Rules that the English followed, though!

As he made this decision, so the two men ducked down by the privies made a break for it, running back towards the hotel. Chilcot took one of them in the back and had the satisfaction of seeing the man go down. This was more like it! Three of those bastards accounted for already and not a scratch on him yet. He hadn't lost any of his old facility with firearms and neither had he, as old men sometimes did, become shaky and indecisive. He'd made his choices and was sticking by them now, come death or high water.

The former sheriff of Grafton Peak was in no hurry to mount any kind of direct assault upon the hotel. It would be madness; he'd be shot down before ever he got there. Chilcot didn't doubt that at this very moment, men were peering out into the night, trying their damnedest to work out what was happening and how many men were attacking the place. How surprised they'd have been to learn that there was just one old man of sixty-six years of age out there, besieging their strong-hold single-handed!

★ ★ ★

Keith Tranter was over in the Golden Eagle, having a quiet drink with one of his cronies. Strange to relate, Sheriff Tranter was by no means unpopular in Grafton's Peak. He had promised to make the town safe for decent folk; a promise which he had, by and large, kept. Even the collection of money from the local businesses was tolerated. The fact was nobody from out of town would give those stores and other locations any aggravation while Tranter's boys were taking an interest in them. The amounts collected were not ruinous; really only enough to pay for the tobacco and liquor which Tranter and his friends used. The aim was certainly not to run them into the ground. For most in town, Tranter was a pretty tough customer who made sure that folk could live their lives peacefully and make a profit from the activities in which he had a hand. Grafton's Peak put up with Keith Tranter because it was to their long-term advantage to do so. Almost everybody in town knew about Tranter's parentage, but most folk didn't much care, just as long as he carried on keeping things quiet and profitable for them.

'Where the devil has Catesby got to?' said Tranter irritably. 'I told him to meet us here at nine.'

'Ah, you know what he's like,' said Tom Fowler. 'Chasing tail or something of that nature. He'll be here.'

They supped their whiskey for a space in companionable silence and then Tranter observed quietly, 'I'm right looking forward to killing that Chilcot.'

'What in the hell made him come back here, d'you suppose?'

'I wouldn't know,' said Tranter. 'It's a Godsend for me. I promised him when I was no more than a kid that I'd kill him one day and now's the time. Ain't it funny how things work out?'

Fowler, who had never really considered the point before, nodded in agreement. Then he said, 'Don't mind me sayin', but we need to ease back on the payments from the lumber mill. Owner's going to be cuttin' up rough directly.'

'Take less,' said Tranter at once, 'or leave it for a week or two. Long as they know they got to pay something, that's the main thing. We ain't none of us going to get rich and retire on the nickels and dimes coming in from those places. Just so they 'member who's running the town and who they owe.'

It was at this point that Tranter and Fowler heard an excited man at the bar telling anybody who would listen that there was a shootout taking place right that second down at the depot. Tranter stood up and sauntered casually over to the bar. 'What's this about shooting?'

'There's some sort of fight going on by the Commercial, Sheriff. Nobody knows what's happenin'.'

'Next time you hear of such a thing,'

said Tranter mildly, 'you be sure and inform your sheriff before you tell some barkeep. Is that clear?'

'Yeah, of course. Sorry, I didn't think — '

'Well now, if you don't think, then happen you ought to keep your mouth closed.'

There seemed no sort of reply to this and so the man said nothing, thinking that Sheriff Tranter was a little out of sorts and it didn't look like the best time to get crosswise to him.

Chilcot was feeling foxed about the best course of action to take now. He had dealt with three of the men who were in the Commercial, but the rest were evidently not minded to venture outside. He could hardly fire at the windows randomly, for fear of hitting any of the girls in the building. It was a regular conundrum that was solved when he saw that a man with a rifle was lurking in one of the rooms where the lamps had been wholly extinguished. Could he take this man with a pistol at a distance of forty or fifty feet? Chilcot was quite confident that he could.

At no time at all had Chilcot allowed himself to be seen by any of those in the Commercial, who consequently had no idea whether they were fighting against one man or a dozen. This perhaps accounted for the curious climax and resolution to what later became known in Grafton's Peak as 'The Second Shootout at the Depot'.

Sheriff Tranter and his friend Fowler approached the Commercial from the depot, where they had been told that the shooting was taking place. Everything seemed utterly quiet as they crossed the railroad tracks and came closer to the hotel. The only unusual circumstance was that most of the hotel's rooms appeared to be in darkness. This was odd, because it was only ten o'clock and in the general way of things the Commercial was lively enough on any night of the week. It was especially odd tonight because of course there were a bunch of girls staying over there for a while, along with the men who were escorting them south to the border. Tranter would have expected to hear the cheerful tones of the piano, as well as much laughing and perhaps singing. What the hell was going on? At that moment came two shots in quick succession, one of which sent Tom Fowler sprawling in the cinders. Tranter saw the flash from one of the darkened windows at back of the Commercial. He drew his gun and began returning fire.

It had been a matter for Chilcot of watching that figure hovering behind the window. He felt sure that he could take the man out if he would only stand still for a second. At last, the shadowy figure up on the first floor did stop moving and the rifle could be plainly seen. The window was open and it was obvious that this fellow was searching for a target. Chilcot took careful aim and fired. The man in the window fell back, although whether because he had been hit or perhaps due to his having thrown himself down in alarm at being shot at, it was impossible to tell. Almost at once, somebody in the next window opened fire, although not at Chilcot. This person had heard the shot and, looking from the window at that moment had seen two men creeping towards the back of the hotel. Taking them for attackers, he fired at once, wounding Tom Fowler. It was at this point that Sheriff Tranter began shooting towards the Commercial.

Observing all this with enormous pleasure, Chilcot calculated that his best move now was to sit back and let whoever had now appeared shoot it out with the men in the hotel. He continued to crouch behind the wall, enjoying the spectacle of various men trading shots with each other. He just hoped that those girls were keeping well away from the windows.

Tranter had taken up a position behind the privies and every so often he would lean out and fire at one or other of the windows at back of the hotel. All the lamps had now been extinguished and his shots were not likely to find any targets. The sheriff could not for the life of him work out what was going on and why the men in that building should be trying to kill him. Those in the Commercial had now identified the threat that they faced and decided that it came from a group of men hiding towards the railroad tracks who were mounting an assault against the hotel for the Lord only knew what reason. The men in the hotel sent bullets flying towards the privies, keeping what they believed to be a party of gunmen pinned down there.

There was a lull in the firing and Tranter called out, 'You men in there, you best throw down your weapons and come out with your hands in the air.'

There was dead silence and then somebody shouted into the night, 'Tranter? Is that you?'

All at once, the state of affairs dawned on Sheriff Tranter, because he called back, 'Farnham, is that you, you bastard? What the hell do you think you're doing, shooting at me?' Keith Tranter was a shrewd and resourceful man, but at this point he made a rare and unaccustomed mistake. Having established that this whole thing was in the nature of a foolish misunderstanding, he stepped out from where he had been sheltering and showed himself to those looking out of the Commercial's windows. One of those watching was a Mexican, whose grasp of the English language was exceedingly tenuous. He hadn't understood much of the shouted exchange between Sheriff Tranter and the fellow leaning out of the hotel window and so simply fired when he had a good view of the man below. Keith Tranter, sheriff of Grafton's Peak, fell back with a bullet hole slap bang between his eyes.

11

After seeing Ike Adams's boy die, Chilcot kind of figured that there was no point hanging around the scene any further. Including Catesby, who he assumed had been in some sense Tranter's righthand man, six of Tranter's men were now lying dead. Of course, most importantly of all, their boss was dead too. That day probably saw the end of the crooked rule over Grafton's Peak. Unless the citizens were foolish enough to install another badman sheriff, then things would perhaps grow a little healthier now.

In any case, Chilcot felt that he had done as much as one man could be expected to do. Then he thought that there might be just one more little task to undertake, although not an arduous one. Crowds of interested people were now drifting towards the depot and

Chilcot didn't particularly wish to be called upon to explain and justify his own part in the shootout. Others could try to unravel the business if they had a mind to do so. He set off back towards Main Street.

It took Chilcot a little while to find the alleyway down which Catesby had conducted him earlier that day. Eventually, he found it and when he slipped through the door, it looked very much as though nobody had been there since he had himself left. It was his idea that these two mean little rooms were some sort of centre of operations for Tranter and his men. There were ledgers and files piled neatly in the back room where he had first seen Sheriff Tranter. Some were on the table; others were lined up on a bookshelf. Chilcot took as many as he could carry and then left the room, dropping Catesby's pistol next to his body. He also tossed to the floor the gun which he'd taken from the Mexican.

It was almost eleven when Chilcot

returned to the Pearsons' house. Lights were still burning downstairs and Mrs Pearson opened the door almost the instant he knocked upon it. 'Mr Chilcot,' she said, 'we've been so worried. There's been gunfire across towards the depot. We were standing outside with our neighbour and listening to it. I thought of you.'

Jake appeared at the top of the stairs. The boy was dressed for bed, but there was no indication that he was prepared to sleep right now. His mother glanced up the stairs and said sharply, 'Jacob, you'll be the death of me. You know fine well that you've to be up early tomorrow morning to be getting back to that school of yours. Was ever a mother plagued with a more disobedient son?'

'Can I come down and hear what Mr Chilcot has been about?'

'Lord, you might just as well, I suppose. Do you promise me that you'll go straight back to bed and try to sleep if I give you leave now to come and exchange a few words?'

'I promise, Ma.'

'Well then, come down now. I'll set some coffee on the stove. I dare say you could do with a cup, Mr Chilcot?'

'It'd be most welcome, ma'am.'

When they went into the kitchen, Chilcot set the armful of ledgers down on the table. 'What're they, sir?' asked Jake.

'I don't rightly know, son. I picked them up earlier. I've not had a chance to look through them yet.'

'May I look at them?' asked Jake.

'You are the worst boy as ever I knew,' said Mrs Pearson. 'Are you not ashamed to set your nose in other folk's affairs like this? I'm sorry, Mr Chilcot. I don't know what's come over that son of mine lately and that's a fact.'

Chilcot chuckled. 'I was a boy of that age myself, once upon a time, ma'am. It was long ago, but I recall how inquisitive I was about everything going on around me.' He turned to Jake. 'Go ahead, son. It looks to me to be mainly figures and ciphering. I got the idea when I saw your schoolbooks that you were a whale at that kind of work. If you can tell me anything worth knowing about these books, I'll be in your debt.'

While Chilcot and Mrs Pearson drank their coffee, Jake pored over the leather-bound volumes. At length he said, 'I think I see what's what, but I could be wrong.'

'Go on,' said Chilcot. 'How'd you read them?'

'Looks to me as if these are accounts or book-keeping or something of the sort. But whoever's kept 'em has made two records of the same dates, but entering different amounts in each. That's about all I can say.'

The old man smiled cheerfully and reached over to clap young Jake on the shoulder. 'I should think that you have the case read right,' he said. 'Could it be that that somebody was keeping a true set of records and a duplicate, with false figures?'

'I guess so,' said the boy, 'but I can't see why anybody would do such a thing.'

'Suppose you were stealing money from a company or even a town,' said Chilcot. 'You'd want to know for yourself how things stood in the finance line, but also you'd want to guy it up so nobody else could see the true state of affairs. You understand?'

At this point, Mrs Pearson broke in indignantly, 'You mean to tell me that that sheriff was robbing the town, just like he was storekeepers and such?'

Chilcot laughed out loud at her outrage. 'It's not all that uncommon, ma'am. A lot o' towns have money siphoned off by dishonest means. There's a deal of graft and corruption around. Would have been surprisin' to me if somewhat of the kind hadn't been taking place.'

Mrs Pearson turned to her son and said, 'Come on, Jacob, it's long past your time to be in bed. You've an early start in the morning.'

The boy yawned. 'It's surely been an exciting time having you around, sir,' he said to Chilcot. 'I hope you'll come and visit with us sometime, during the school break.'

'Who knows what the future holds?' said Chilcot. 'Let's get the next few days out of the way, before we begin wondering about the summer.'

After Jake had gone up to bed, Chilcot said, 'You have a sound young fellow there, ma'am. He's got all the makings of a good man. A clever one too, if I'm any judge o' them things.'

'What will you do now, Mr Chilcot? That wretched son of mine dragged you down here and it's nearly cost you your life. You won't be rushing back to Kansas just yet awhile?'

'I hope to leave tomorrow afternoon, if you won't object to my spending one more night under your roof. What's worse is that I'm obliged to ask you for the loan of the price of the railroad ticket. I'll send you the money when I get back to Endurance.'

'You're very welcome to the money, of course. But what I wondered was if you would care to stay on here for a while? It would be a pleasure to have you and I know that Jacob would be pleased.'

To his mortification, Chilcot felt his eyes prickling and his vision was obscured by the rainbow flashes that gave him cause to suppose that in another minute, he might actually start crying. To cover his confusion, he pulled out a handkerchief and said, 'I have some piece of grit in my eye. Excuse me a moment.' He left the room and fiddled around in front of the looking glass in the front parlour. Then he blew his nose and rejoined Mrs Pearson. 'What were we talking of?' he said.

'I asked if you would care to stay on here for a spell.'

'It's right kind of you, ma'am. Truth to tell, there's nothing would please me more, but I have to be getting back. I'd like to visit, though, maybe in the summer?'

'You'll always be very welcome here, Mr Chilcot. And my offer remains open.'

When he'd bid Jake's mother good-night, Chilcot took a turn round the garden to clear his head. The events of the day were catching up on him now and he ached all over. He'd seen more action in the last forty-eight hours than in the five previous years.

He thought about that marvellous offer from Mrs Pearson. He was immensely touched, but knew that it wouldn't answer. He was reaching an age soon when he might not be able to care entirely for himself and he was damned if he was going to see Jake and his mother burdened with a helpless old man. Nor did he feel inclined to become a charity case, if it came to that. No, he would do well enough on his own.

That little pension of his was adequate to cover his food and lodging, as well as the livery bills for his horse. What had been driving him to destitution was the habit of spending most days in the saloon. Since meeting Jake Pearson, he'd not touched a drop of liquor and what's more had hardly felt the lack of it. He really thought that he might be off the stuff altogether and for good. It was all well and good for the Pearsons to make out that he'd been some sort of help to them, but from where he was sitting, it looked to Chilcot as though the boot was all on the other foot. It was they who had rescued him.

Chilcot was up bright and early the next morning to see young Jake off to school. He walked down to the depot with the boy and his mother to wave him goodbye. They passed the Commercial, where crowds were still hanging round, trying to work out what had happened there. He remarked to Mrs Pearson, 'I've a notion that the town's goin' to be a little more careful about the next person they choose for sheriff. They might want somebody who's a little less apt to get mixed up with the bad fellows.'

'You might have a point. Do you think that it will become widely known that Keith Tranter was 'cooking the books', as the saying goes?'

'You know, ma'am, I have a strong idea that it will be the talk of the town in no time at all.'

Mrs Pearson gave him a sidelong glance.

Before Jake boarded the train which would take him to school, Chilcot shook his hand and said, 'I earnestly entreat you to pay attention to your studies, boy. Take it from one who knows, that's a surer path to fortune and success than fooling around with firearms.'

'Thank you, sir. Thank you for everything.'

Suspecting, quite correctly, that Mrs Pearson would wish for some time to make her own farewells to her son, Chilcot said, 'Might I beg the favour of the keys to your house, ma'am? I have an errand to run, but I'll be sure to be back there in time so you won't arrive locked out of your own abode.'

As soon as he left the depot, Chilcot walked briskly back to the Pearson house, let himself in and collected together the ledgers which he had taken after Catesby's death. He then went off at a similarly fast pace to Main Street and slipped down the little alleyway where Keith Tranter had kept his secret office. The door to the two little rooms was closed and there was no sign that anybody had yet found Catesby's body.

Chilcot slipped through the door and closed it behind him. He went into the back room, carted all the books and ledgers out and strewed them on the very threshold of the door opening onto the alleyway. That was the easy bit. He then set to dragging Catesby's corpse to the same location. The dead man was a considerable weight and Chilcot found himself panting with the exertions and running with sweat by the time that he had finally manhandled the corpse to where he wanted it. So far, so good.

He would need to sit a while and

gather his strength, because the next action would have to be done pretty smartly and he would have to use all his strength at once. Everything was in place. He opened the door a crack and peered out. There was nobody to be seen. Chilcot grabbed hold of Catesby and dragged him out, so that the dead man lay sprawled across the alleyway with his legs still in the room. For good measure, Chilcot piled a few of the account books on the corpse's legs and then walked off rapidly.

It surely wouldn't take long for the body of Tranter's lieutenant to be found and the false accounts with them. That should just about put the lid on the dead sheriff's reputation.

Parting from Jake's mother later, Chilcot said, 'I'll be taking you up on your offer of coming to visit this summer, ma'am. You may depend upon it.'

'I'm glad to hear it, Mr Chilcot. Your visit here was short and, if I might use the expression, bloody. But I think that things might get a little better in Grafton's Peak before long.'

As he settled down in his seat on the train to the junction, Brook Chilcot knew that his life had changed for good and all. He'd not touched a drop of ardent spirits since that first meeting with the boy and if he was any judge of such things, he never would again. He felt in some obscure way that the action of the last few days had in some way cancelled out the past and he was looking forward to making the very most of what life there was remaining to him. Chilcot wasn't a man to believe overmuch in reformation or redemption, but in as much as such things were possible, he thought that he had, as a consequence of the events in Grafton's Peak this last week, reformed himself. He was looking forward with relish to the rest of his life.

We do hope that you have enjoyed reading this large print book.

Did you know that all of our titles are available for purchase?

We publish a wide range of high quality large print books including:
Romances, Mysteries, Classics
General Fiction
Non Fiction and Westerns

Special interest titles available in large print are:
The Little Oxford Dictionary
Music Book, Song Book
Hymn Book, Service Book

Also available from us courtesy of Oxford University Press:
Young Readers' Dictionary
(large print edition)
Young Readers' Thesaurus
(large print edition)

For further information or a free brochure, please contact us at:
Ulverscroft Large Print Books Ltd.,
The Green, Bradgate Road, Anstey,
Leicester, LE7 7FU, England.
Tel: (00 44) **0116 236 4325**
Fax: (00 44) **0116 234 0205**

TWO GUNS NORTH

Neil Hunter

Jason Brand's latest assignment takes him into the mountains, searching for two missing men — a Deputy US Marshal and a government geologist. But this apparently routine assignment turns out to be anything but. For Bodie the Stalker, hunting a brutal killer, rides the same trail. It's just another manhunt for him — until he finds himself on the wrong end of the chase. But then Bodie meets Brand. And when they join forces, it's as if Hell itself has come to the high country . . .

GUNS OF THE BRASADA

Neil Hunter

Ballard and McCall are in Texas, working for Henry Conway, an old friend, on the Lazy-C ranch. But trouble is brewing: Yancey Merrick, owner of the big Diamond-M, kept pushing to expand his empire. Then Henry's son Harry is run down through the brasada thicket before being shot in the back and killed. Determined to find the guilty party, Ballard and McCall suddenly find themselves deep in a developing range war . . .

LONELY RIDER

Steve Hayes

He calls himself 'Melody', after the word burned inside his belt. Because he can't remember his own name — or anything at all prior to the past six weeks. It's 'amnesia', according to Regan Avery, the woman he rescues from a fast-flowing river. But Melody doesn't need the fancy name for his predicament to know he's in trouble — for the few things he *can* remember involve being shot at and wounded, with a posse hard on his heels . . .